First Edition

FINDING MY PERFECT

The VanByrne Boys

Norma Burdette

To all the readers who need to know, there is always a perfect waiting for you. It's never too late in life to find your perfect.

PROLOGUE

"Disrobe and stand by the window, clutching the pearls in your teeth. We will start there and slowly have you look out at the skyline. Try not to pout this time, we need a few good shots for Marco to get the ad out."

It seems like I get the same type of clients over and over. No one wants to be creative anymore. All these big companies think it's only the beautiful people and sex that sell their product. I am bored out of my mind shooting these beautiful people at all hours of the day just to capture the one shot. I am not even sure I can keep this up without losing my mind or self respect. When I became a photographer I wanted to capture what no one else saw, now I want to capture anything else.
Forty years of this life and I am ready to just toss it all away, before I crack. I thought this life was going to change the way the world saw beauty but what it changed was me and how I documented it.

"Molly, can you turn slightly while letting the pearls drop to the floor?" God this is beginning to kill me slowly from the inside. I need a break from all this madness.

"That's it, now turn your head towards me and look lost but don't raise your eyes up." I swear these same shots are requested by everyone. Can no one be creative? Give them what they want and enjoy the comforts of life. I think I am done with comforts, I am done with perfect!

"I got it, thanks Molly. You are done, I will send you a few copies for your portfolio as always."

"Raya, cancel all my shoots for the next two weeks so my schedule is clear. I need to go visit my sister and I don't need any complaints. Man the phones while I am gone and you still get paid." I was becoming an asshole, no, I was an asshole. I am so frustrated with where I am in life that I am treating people I care about like shit. This wasn't me, this was not what I wanted out of life.

Life was short, there is no reason why I was becoming a heartless ass. I had a good life, I was healthy and had more money than I would ever need. It was the happy that was missing from the equation, I just wasn't happy. Hell, I hadn't been happy for more years than I could count.
There was a time in my life that I thought I could have it all. I would get my career going, find a beautiful woman and create a great life. A life that involved children and the one woman who could love me, like my brother had.

The perfect life my brother had was short lived but he got to taste it. His wife was devoted to him, he had great kids and a job he loved. Hell, until his fatal heart attack I was completely jealous of him. He found it all and was so damn happy. Then one day the phone rings and life as we all knew it stopped, it just stopped.

Letty was a broken woman when my brother died. She lost her

one true love and I had to be there to help her survive. After years of watching her and making sure she was ok, I was now watching my life crumble. Letty was my only connection to my brother, well his children were there too. I always thought of her as a sister and when her life fell apart, I did what my brother would have wanted, I took care of his family.

Seeing your only brother leave this earth so young makes you take a hard look yourself. I started to focus on my health, I needed to stick around for Letty in case she needed anything. I became obsessed with working out, correct nutrition and lots of medical screening so I didn't leave like Arthur did.
The only draw back to all this?
I forgot to live, I forgot to reap the rewards of the life I had built.

Now I was approaching 70 with no children, no legacy and no one to come home to every day. I was alone in the busiest damn city in the world and fed up with the shallow, beautiful people that surrounded me. I needed a break or I was going to have a breakdown in spite of my impeccable health.

"Raya, I need a flight for Colorado and a rental car ready when I land. The sooner I head out the better."

"Will you be needing any accommodations while you are there? Any hotel preferences or cabins I can rent?" Raya could see his frustration and was doing all the bookings as she spoke.

"I won't be needing a place, I just need a flight and a car. Let me know when it's set, I will be packing upstairs waiting on the details."

This break can't come soon enough!

I can't keep barking at Raya, she is just doing her job. She has been my assistant for years and never wavered, not even when she married and started her own family. I really need to get away and regroup before she reaches her breaking point.

"August, I have a cab on the way. Your flight leaves in two hours no stops or layovers, I have an SUV reserved at the airport once you land. I have your usual travel cash ready and your ticket printed out. Is there anything else I can do for you before you head out?"

"Raya, I am an ass. You are a gem for dealing with my bullshit and I want you to take the next two weeks for your family. Get a service to take all our calls and enjoy your family. You have full access to my beach house and the staff there. Spend the time with your family and try to forgive me for all my faults. I will expect you back, fully rested and relaxed once I return, not before. Take your children to the beach and enjoy the sun."

I threw my bag over my shoulder and let the elevator carry me down to the lobby. The cab was at the curb as soon as I left the building, Raya was that good.

I would use my flight to work on my photos and email out the last of my shots. My two weeks at Letty's was going to be work free, nothing but relaxing in natures beauty. This was exactly what I needed to get my shit together.

CHAPTER 1

"Letty, I told you I am not going to have tea with your brother in law. I am not interested in getting to know any man, I have a full life with these boys and these kittens running the house."

"Emma, you are going to go down in history as the lonely, crazy cat lady. I have to catch a flight to Georgia, my granddaughter is ready to arrive and August is in the air now. I need you to give him the key to my house and just show him around. He just wants to relax and enjoy the slow life for the next two weeks. If Amy wasn't in labor now I would wait on him. You know I would do the same for you! Just please promise me you will, I need to go if I am going to catch my flight."

"Fine, but I am doing this under protest, you hear me? I do not need to be spending my time babysitting some spoiled city boy. I suppose I could invite him to dinner since he probably hasn't had real food in a while. You know those big cities only serve tiny portions of organic kale stuff made into art right? Who on earth eats pretty art on a bamboo saucer and calls it dinner?"

"Oh for heavens sake Emma, they have real food there too. Every time I visited him we went to good restaurants but he could probably use your home cooking just the same. Look, I need to run now but I love you dearly and thank you again for doing this. You still have my spare key at your house right? I will call you when I get to hold that little princess and let you know when I will be coming back."

"Yes, I have your key hanging on the hook in the office. Have a nice visit, bring back as much of that sweet Georgia produce as you can carry and we will call it even. I have dinner to get ready and then check on Rachel. That poor girl is still not feeling well but she has an appointment in the morning with Brian so he will get to the bottom of it. Give Amy a hug from me and take lots of pictures." Granny hung up the phone and headed to the kitchen. She was going to make Rachel homemade soup and some lemon tea. Rachel had been writing away on her new book series, so she was spending a lot of time upstairs.

"Granny can you come help me get these kittens out of the office please? I don't know why they feel the need to sneak in here, they have a jungle of toys in the den." Mikey was carrying two little kittens but still had three more to evict. Granny had placed little colored bow ties with names on each of them so she could keep them straight. The two little boys were blessed with black tufts of hair on top their heads making it clear which ones were going to be trouble. The remaining three were little girls and mostly bald with the exception of Cleo, she had calico striped fur around all four paws. She seemed to be the leader of the mischief crew and was also the fastest one when she wanted to be.

"Cleo, Leo, Ling, Mac and Jac where are you sweet babies? Granny has treats for you!" Granny called from the kitchen while shaking the treat jar. In true pied piper form, the little feline gang filed into the kitchen from all directions.

"Now you little sweethearts know you can't bother Mikey while he is working. Get back to the den and play nice." Granny directed as the tiny mafia headed to the den where Lu and Guido were lounging in the sun. Granny had a gift with these little misfits but it WAS Granny after all. Just like those VanByrne boys, when Granny spoke, you listened.

As Granny headed back to the kitchen she heard the front doorbell ring and abruptly ring again. Not expecting anyone so soon, Granny made her way back to the front of the house curious as to who was so persistent.

"I swear whoever is working that bell like an elevator button better need help or they may just……" Granny stopped talking as soon as she got the door open. There, standing on her front porch, was a tall chiseled man with the whitest hair that held a messy cut dripping across his forehead. He also had a very well groomed beard to match his beautiful hair. His tanned skin looked to be dusted in gold and the bluest crystals for eyes that looked into her soul. Sweet baby Jesus, this man was at the wrong house but she did not mind the visual break her eyes were taking.

"Is this the Brewer house? I was told I could stop by to see Emma and get a key?" August was hesitant to speak, thinking he had the wrong house. Letty had told him that Emma was in her 70's but the woman who came to the door looked to be a natural woman in her 50's. Maybe this was a daughter or a guest in this establishment? She was clearly fit with a petite hourglass shape, not like the thin shapeless females he usually saw. Her eyes were lined with years of smiles that never saw a scalpel. This woman was beautiful without any makeup and her shoulder length blonde hair showed wisps of silver, clearly un-tampered with as well.

"I am August Wander and you are?"

"I am who you are looking for...... I mean, I am Emma Brewer. Come in, please. I have Letty's key in the back office." Emma walked back toward the kitchen to grab the key and turn down the stove. August followed her through the house, taking in all the charm of this beautiful, old home.

"That smells amazing, you must be a wonderful cook." I could not sound more pathetic but in my defense, I do not cook, I microwave or let a chef cook for me. Whatever was on that stove smelled like my grandma's kitchen and my childhood. A simple smell could take me back to a much simpler time and get me all nostalgic, I needed to snap out of it.

"It's just some soup I whipped up for lunch if you would like to stay? I have some toasted sandwiches to go with it and you are more than welcome. I will warn you though, this house gets crazy." Emma was nervous and was definitely feeling eyes on her. Had this man never seen a older woman before, one free of Botox?

"I don't want to impose on your family, I need to get settled in at Letty's anyway. I can grab a bite to eat in town but thank you." I would love to stay and sample this amazing food. Why do I always shut everyone out? Eating alone sucks and eating out is depressing.

"Nonsense, I told Letty I would take care of you in her absence. If you leave I will have lied to my very best friend. Can you bear that burden? Forcing an old woman to lie to her best friend?" Emma was laying it on thick but it looked like she had to. This beautiful slice of man meat was actually going to pass on her cooking. No one had ever passed on her cooking. She also just needed to appreciate his gorgeous features for a little bit longer. What in heavens name had gotten in to her?

"You just talked me into it. I just have to run my bags over to the house and I will be right back. Can I bring anything?"

What?

What could I possibly contribute to this lunch? I do not cook, I do not have any notable culinary skills to offer and I have only been on the ground an hour. I must be jet lagged because I was starting to sound pretty simple.

"You just bring yourself back and we will all share a meal. Oh and August? We are just simple, happy folks here so no need to dress up for lunch." Emma winked at August and shot him a sweet smile.

"Thank you and I will be back shortly but please don't hold anything up for me. I am a pretty low maintenance man and don't mind eating leftovers." August winked back at Emma as he headed for the door.

What in the world is going on here? August Wander just winked at me! He is just a photographer but my gracious, he could be

on the other end of the camera with that rugged handsome-
ness! Now he is coming back to my house full of chaos to eat at
my table! Why am I freaking out over this? I am a 72 year old
woman for gods sake! I am not some 20 year old doe eyed girl. I
am going to make Letty pay for this when she gets back in town.
I do not have time to be all swoony right now.
Oh no, Rachel!
I need to feed that girl before she wastes away!
This man is already creating disruptions and he has only just
arrived!

CHAPTER 2

"Granny, thank you for the soup it smells amazing. I was hoping to come down and enjoy a meal with everyone but I need to get this book finished. I also need to work on wedding plans and enjoy a little bit of the last days of summer. Is Nate back yet?" Nate had been working lots of hours training the new group of rookies on water rescue. It was something he was very skilled at, so training young recruits was very rewarding.

"He isn't back yet but I will send him on up when he gets here. How are you feeling? You look like you have lost 10 pounds this week, tomorrow can't come soon enough. Are you sure you don't want me to go with you? I don't mind and I could take you to lunch after, a girls day?"

"Granny, you are so sweet but Nate is supposed to have tomorrow off and was adamant I let him come along. Some days I think he is overly protective of me but I must admit, it feels good. I just wish I could shake this bug, I do not have time for this. I promise I will tell you everything when I get back tomorrow though." Rachel spoke to Granny over her shoulder as she headed back upstairs. Rachel was worried about what she may find out at Brian's office. It is going to be strange having her future brother in law give her an exam but with her new, not so great insurance, he was giving her a family discount.

Rachel was pulled from her thoughts as her cell phone began playing "Burning". Nate was constantly changing her ringtone to make her smile. Rachel saw Nate's name on the screen and smiled as she answered.

"Hello handsome, you better not be telling me your stuck at work again."

"Rachel, it's Captain."

Why was Captain using Nate's phone? What is going on?

"Captain? Why are you calling from Nate's phone? Is Nate ok?"

"Rachel there was an issue with the training, we are at the hospital. You should probably head down here but please don't tell Granny yet. I don't want to worry her."

"Captain you are worrying me! What is going on? Is Nate ok? Please tell me he is ok!"

"Rachel I just need you down here, can you do that? Do I need to send a car to get you?"

"Umm no, I am leaving now! Please tell me he is ok!"

"Rachel, just get here! I have got to go, I am needed....."

Rachel had made her way to the car but found herself shaking as she attempted to start it. The key was not turning and her eyes were beginning to blur with tears. Praying that Nate was ok and attempting to start the car took everything she had. She didn't see the gentleman until a tap on her window drew her attention.

"Miss, are you ok? Can I help you?"

"Hospital, I need to get to the hospital but my damn car won't start! I need to hurry but I can't do it!" Heavy sobs wracked Rachel's frail body.

"I was coming for lunch but let me drive you. My SUV is right here and I can get you there safely. You are in no condition to drive dear. I promise you, I will get you there. My name is August Wander, Letty's brother in law, let me help you."

"Ok, thank you."

August loaded Rachel into his SUV and sped toward the hospital. He remembered it well and felt his stomach drop as he pulled into the parking lot.

"I think I need to park and help you go in. Do you know where you are going? What area or floor? We can just go into the ER if we need to."

"ER! I need to go there, I think."

"Ok, let's go in and start there."

August held Rachel up as they walked into the ER. There were several firefighters gathered in the waiting area. A couple of them turned and looked up as the large glass doors flew open. Paul was one of the firefighters Rachel had met when she arrived in town and saw him approaching.
"Rachel, it's Nate. We had a training drill at the lake and some-

how an airbag deployed in the car. Rachel he is in back and we haven't heard anything. The battery wasn't supposed to be in the car, this should not have happened."

Oh god no! Nate was too big and too strong to be hurt! This is a bad dream, it has to be! There is no way this man would come into my life and own my soul, just to be ripped away! He has to be ok, he has to be!

"Rachel, you need to sit down you look like you are going to drop!" August reached for Rachel as she leaned forward and fell into his arms.

"Nurse! We need to get someone out here, now!" August was carrying Rachel to a gurney staged nearby. There was more to this than fainting, Rachel was cold and clammy with no color in her face.

"I need to get her to a room, does she have a name?" Dr. Manuel was rushing to the gurney with a nurse right behind her.

"This is Rachel, Nate's fiancé. Nate was brought in with head, neck injury from the training drill. Please help Rachel!" Paul was rubbing his head and neck pacing, unsure what was happening.

"She is in good hands, we will get her in back and find out what's going on." Dr. Manuel knew Nate was Brian's brother, she was waiting to call him until she had more information. The injury could be very serious but the test results weren't back yet.

"Should I alert Emma or go pick her up? Rachel lives there and I am sure she will be worried."

"I am sorry, who are you?" Paul was confused by this stranger and who Emma was.

"I am August Wander, I was at Emma's when Rachel was trying to drive here alone. I saw she was upset and took it upon myself to get her here safely. Do I need to alert Emma? The house she was at?"

"Granny? No we do not want to worry Granny yet. Not until we know something." It all began to make sense now. Emma was Granny but no one in town knew her by Emma. Everyone had just always called her Granny, even Paul.
"I am sorry, I am Paul. I was with Nate when the accident happened, which is why Rachel is here. We need to wait until the doctor comes back out before we call Granny or Brian. I guess now for both Nate and Rachel."

"I do not feel right staying here with Emma not knowing. I think I should head back to Emma's and wait for the call. You will call her, correct?" August was thinking back to his brother and what it did to Letty. He did not like the fact that they were keeping this from Emma but it wasn't his place to tell her, was it?

"I promise we will have them call her first. Until we know what's going on we have nothing to tell her. She will be mad as hell but for now, it's best she not worry." Paul was praying that the news would be good.

August nodded and thought briefly about leaving his number with Paul but decided that would be too intrusive. August walked through the automatic doors and into the parking lot. Pausing at the door to his SUV, August looked back at the hospital doors, memories were weighing heavy on his mind.

The drive back to Emma's house seemed to take hours. How was he supposed to keep quiet on everything he knew. Emma would be furious if he was not honest with her. He was too new in town to compile enemies, especially one as beautiful as Emma. Sure he was only here for a couple weeks but there was no doubt he hoped to visit more often. Letty was family and he needed to stay connected with family or risk dying a lonely asshole.

CHAPTER 3

"Sorry Granny but Gabby and I are going to miss lunch. We have to meet with the minister today for our classes. The church is available for our fall wedding plans so we need to stick to the schedule the minister sent us. You understand, right?" Mikey felt terrible for missing another lunch. He and Gabby were so busy getting their wedding set that everything else took a back seat. Granny knew how important this was to him so she handled the news well.

"Of course Mikey! You and Gabby are doing so well with all this, just don't forget I am available to help out. If you need me for anything I can jump right in and handle it."

"I know Granny and we love you for that but Gabby is trying to make this part of our new journey. It's been pretty smooth so far but it's good to know we have you as back up." Mikey kissed Granny on the cheek and headed out the door. He had to get to Gabby's so they could head to the church together and on time.

The doorbell rang as Mikey grabbed the handle of the front door. August was waiting on the porch to be invited in.

"Granny expecting you I presume?" Mikey looked August up and down as Granny walked up behind him.

"Mikey I raised you better than that, now apologize for being rude to our guest!"

"My apologies sir, I was just on my way out. Please come in and make yourself at home." Mikey could feel his grandmother staring holes in the back of his head. If he didn't need to meet Gabby he was ready to turn right back around and stay for lunch. This guy was too young to be eyeing up Granny like she was on the menu. Mikey was calling a family meeting when he finished up with his class, this was not happening.

"Please come in August, it would seem my entire family has abandoned me today. Are you hungry? I have plenty of soup and sandwiches in the kitchen, I even have a lovely blueberry pie, fresh from the oven, for dessert." Granny was clearly nervous but hoping August could not tell.
"I am starving actually but I feel I should tell you something first."

Oh my word, he thinks I am hitting on him! He probably has a harem of women in his fancy New York penthouse just waiting on his return. I am far too old to be interested in him or his lifestyle no matter how captivating his eyes or strong jawline are.

"I am sorry, did I give you the wrong impression? It's just lunch but you can take it to go if you would like." Granny was walking toward the kitchen as she spoke. This was both terrifying and humiliating at the same time. Did she stare too long? God he was easy to lose yourself in. I can just get some containers out of the cabinet and bundle him a few meals. He could even take the whole pie, my appetite vanished as soon as he said "but", lord help me.

"No Emma, please let me explain. That girl, Rachel? Was outside trying to start her car when I arrived the first time but was very upset. I drove her to the hospital, she said she needed to get to the ER fast. I wanted to tell you because I heard that her fiancé was admitted because of an accident. I thought you should know and I didn't want to…….."

Granny was grabbing her purse and keys as she was speeding out the door.

"Emma, wait! Let me drive you, do not get in a car when you are this upset."
August was running to try and catch Emma before she reached her car.

"Please Emma, let me drive you! I cannot let you leave here like this, come to my SUV and I will drive you. We don't even have to talk, just please let me drive you." Emma nodded and handed her keys to August. She was silent and staring off into nothing as August led her to the front of the house and put her in his passenger seat.

"Emma, I am just belting you in and then I will drive you to the hospital. Just nod your head if you understand what I am saying." Emma nodded in response as tears began to pool in her eyes. August ran around the vehicle and climbed into the drivers seat. As he pulled out onto the street he reached over and squeezed Emma's hand. He wanted to let her know he was going to be there for her. Emma remained transfixed on the street in front of her, praying for the unknown.

Once they arrived at the hospital August parked again and ran around to get Emma out. He was going to make sure she made it inside safely and he was not leaving her side. When they entered the Emergency entrance, Paul was standing in the same place he had been when August left.

Paul looked up as Granny entered and saw the look of heartbreak in her eyes. August was holding onto Granny as they walked toward him.

"Granny there is still no word on Nate. I have been asking every five minutes but there is nothing."

"Paul tell me what happened, I need to know what happened." Granny was leaning into August but looking directly into Pauls eyes.

"We were doing a water rescue simulation where the car was partially submerged. The battery wasn't supposed to be in the car but somehow it was. The back of the car was under water and the engine area wasn't. When Nate and I went in, I focused on the rear seat. I heard the airbag deploy but I didn't realize what happened. I saw Nate fly back and hit the water. I got out as fast as I could Granny but Nate had lost a lot of blood. We got here in less then ten minutes I swear but I haven't heard anything."

"Paul, airbags save lives how could Nate be hurt?"

"Nate was facing the back when it deployed. The cover of the airbag shot out and hit Nate's neck. Granny he was closer than normal and took a direct hit. I don't know how bad it was but it was………bad." Paul was trembling as he recounted the events. Granny reached for Pauls hand and held it to her heart.

"Paul, my Nate is the strongest man I know. He is going to be fine, I can feel it here, in my heart. My boy is going to make it through this, he is too important to this world. August can you help me get answers from the desk?"
August walked with Emma still in his arms to the nurses desk.

"Excuse me, nurse? We need to check on a patient who was brought in here with a neck injury. This is his grandmother and we need to know what is going on."

"Let me check to see if Dr. Manuel is done and I will ask if she can give you an update. Please take a seat and I will be right back."

August led Emma to the line of chairs as the hospital doors slid open. Brian came running to Granny's side.
"Granny I just got a call from Gale, she said Nate was injured and that I should come down. What do you know so far?"

"Nothing, they haven't said anything yet. Brian I cannot have Nate hurt, you hear me? I need you to get your ass back there and help them fix whatever is going on."
Brian nodded in agreement as he made his way to the exam area.

"Gale what's going on? Why has no one spoken to Granny yet? What is the status and can I help?"

"Brian we are waiting on some tests to come back but it looks as though your brother narrowly escaped a spinal cord injury. We are waiting on some images now but I suspect a cervical fracture. We had to close the wound and he is still not awake but there doesn't seem to be any brain trauma. The airbag cover on the steering wheel deployed and hit Nate in the back of his neck slicing him significantly. We are monitoring him closely so if you would like me to speak with Granny I can. I have Rachel in another room, she collapsed in the lobby. She was pretty dehydrated so she is getting fluids while we wait on her blood tests."

"She has been sick and was actually scheduled to come see me in the morning. You stay with Nate, I will update Granny and come back for Rachel. I am her doctor now and until we get Nate's results I can stay busy."

Brian left to update Granny but he would make sure Paul knew too.

"Granny, Nate had a pretty large laceration on the back of his neck. They stopped the bleeding and closed it up. They are running some tests to make sure his spine is ok. He hasn't woken up yet but that is probably for the best. He is resting and not arguing to get out of here. Rachel is in the back as well getting fluids but they are running some blood work on her. I am going to go back and check on Rachel until Nate's tests come back. Until we know more, things seem to be going pretty smooth."

"Brian, I am sorry I yelled at you. I just can't let anything happen to my boys and I hate not knowing. What can I do?"

"Honestly Granny you may want to head back home until we know more. Nate's in good hands and I promise to call as soon as I know more."

"Brian don't make me yell at you twice in one day. I will stay right here and wait but I want to see Nate as soon as I can and Rachel. I want to see Rachel too, so do what you need to but I am not moving from this spot unless it's to see those kids. Understand?"

Brian nodded as he headed back to check on Rachel and look over the tests they had run on her.

CHAPTER 4

"Gabby I don't understand, weren't we supposed to meet the minister today? I specifically cleared my afternoon so we could attend class. Why are you laughing?" Mikey was confused when he walked up the steps at Gabby's house and she wasn't ready.

"Mike I thought we could spend the afternoon here, alone. Our classes actually start next week and before things get hectic, I wanted you to myself." Gabby was blushing as she spoke and looking at her feet.

Even embarrassed and blushing Mikey couldn't stop himself from pulling Gabby to him. Kissing her was like drinking from the purest spring, he couldn't get enough. Since Gabby had come into his life, it was impossible for Mikey to focus on any-thing else when she was near. Today was no exception and now they had the entire afternoon with no distractions.

Mikey's phone ringing in his pocket pulled his attention from Gabby's warm lips. He thought about just ignoring it but saw that it was Brian and answered.

"Hey Brian, what's up?"

After a few moments, Mikey placed the phone back in his

pocket and gave Gabby a lost look.

"Gabby we have to go to the hospital, Nate's been hurt and Rachel collapsed. Brian is there but Granny refuses to leave the waiting room. We need to go sit with her while the doctors take care of Nate." Mikey was scared for what Nate may be facing but Granny needed him there.

"Oh my gosh! We need to go Mike, is he going to be ok? What about Rachel? Poor Granny." Gabby grabbed her purse and met Mikey at his car.

"We should know more once we get there but it sounds like Nate is one lucky guy. Rachel is getting fluids but that's all Brian could tell me."

Gabby and Mikey made it to the ER and found Granny easily. She was leaning on the shoulder of the guy Mikey met earlier. Paul was pacing by the coffee machine rubbing his neck and mumbling to himself. When Mikey reached Granny she looked up from her seated position and tears began to fall.

"Granny they are both going to be ok, they have Brian back there and he would never let anything happen. We just have to be patient and trust that they are both working hard to get through this." Mikey took the seat next to Granny and pulled her into him.

"Granny can I get you anything, are you hungry? Coffee maybe?" Gabby was trying to be helpful while keeping her mind busy. Worrying about Nate and Rachel was not helping anyone.

"I should have had you stop by the house and bring the soup and sandwiches I had made for lunch. I didn't know Brian was going to call you and I know Nate would love some of my soup when he wakes up." Granny was speaking softly as if she was deep in thought. Her mind was on Nate and what this whole ordeal would mean to him and his future.

"Granny I can go and grab those things for you. You all must be starving, I can drive Mike's car and pack everything up." Gabby reached her hand out to Mikey for keys. She was not waiting for any discussion, she knew she could be helpful doing this.

"Gabby I can't ask you to do that, it's too much for one person to do." Granny looked up and saw Paul still pacing looking lost. "Can you ask Paul to go with you and give you a hand? I am certain he is hungry and he is just beating himself up over there." Granny pointed to Paul and looked at Gabby for acknowledgement.

"Sure, we will be back in a bit. Granny they are both going to be fine, I just know it." Gabby took the keys from Mikey and walked over to Paul.

"Paul, Granny has asked that you and I go get some sandwiches from her house. I know you want to stay here but Granny is worried about you. Can you please come with me so she doesn't worry more than she already is?"
Paul looked over at Granny just as she nodded and gave him a weak smile. He saw the pain on her face and knew he needed to get out for a bit. The guilt over the accident had him causing Granny more heartache than she needed.
"Yeah, sure. I can come give you a hand." Paul began walking to

the large entry doors as Gabby smiled at Granny.

Once outside Gabby pointed to Mikey's car and hit the fob to unlock it.

"I would let you drive but I think maybe you just need to ride for a bit. I know your upset about Nate but he is going to be fine Paul. Nate is so healthy and strong there isn't much that can bring him down." Gabby was trying to offer up some comfort to an obviously worried Paul.

As they began the drive, Paul was the first to speak, breaking the silence.

"It was my fault that Nate got hurt, I should have pulled the battery but I overlooked it. My mind wasn't on that drill today and I let something distract me from my job. When it went off.....I just lost it. The noise caught me off guard and I don't think I got to Nate as fast as I should have."

"Paul, they are called accidents for a reason. It wasn't your fault that it happened, if it was a real accident no one would have pulled the battery. Why would you think there is blame to be placed here?"

"Gabby I froze when the bag deployed. I actually froze, I couldn't physically move and I thought I was better, you know? I thought I had beat the demons that haunted me but what happened today......... I didn't beat anything. I thought I could leave all that stuff over there when I got home. I was doing great but this accident brought it all back. What happens if there is another accident where more people than Nate need me? I couldn't live with myself if anything happened to Nate or anyone else for that matter."

Gabby was pulling into Granny's driveway as Paul finished talking. He needed to talk with someone and although she wanted to help him, he needed a professional. Paul needed to get through this and there was no way he could do it alone. Gabby knew she needed to talk to Mike about this. He could help find Paul the right person to get him through this.

"I am glad you talked with me Paul, I am but I think maybe it's time you see a professional. Sometimes what we think is insurmountable is just a blip in our journey. I think if you could talk to someone, who knows what you are experiencing, you may be surprised how far you can come. Will you talk to Mike? He may be able to find the right person for you to talk with."
"I don't know, I want to but this stuff is in my head and I don't think anyone can help me unsee it all. Please keep this between us, I need to think about it. Let's get the food and head back, ok?"

Gabby nodded and used Mike's keys to unlock the door. Paul followed Gabby to the kitchen and began gathering the forgotten food. Gabby wrapped the sandwiches and pulled out styrofoam cups with lids for the soup. Granny had everything they needed to transport the food back to the hospital. Running a bed and breakfast had required she keep all sorts of things on hand. Guests often had to eat on the go and Granny was always making people happy.

"I think we have it all Paul, let's head back. Do you mind carrying the larger box?"

Paul smiled and grabbed both boxes and nodded his head towards the door. He was not one to let any woman carry something he was more than capable of carrying. This trip with Gabby helped him shake the events of the morning from his head. He just needed to make sure Nate was ok, he prayed that Nate was ok.

CHAPTER 5

"Rachel, I need to talk to you about your tests. We have them all back now and the sooner we go over them, the sooner we can check on Nate." Brian was very concerned with Nate's condition especially now that he had Rachel's results.

"Please Brian, give it to me straight so I can go see Nate."

"I see an elevated white cell count but that can be brought on by stress. It's not alarming, we may need to run another screen but I am also showing a higher level of HCG. Rachel do you know when your last menstrual cycle was?"

"Oh God, Brian I don't remember, it has been so crazy these last few weeks. I was getting the depo shot but since I changed insurance and my house burned I just…….let it slip. Brian am I pregnant? Is that why I have been so sick?"

"First off, let's calm down. The test does indicate that you could very well be pregnant but to be certain we could do an ultrasound. If you want to know for certain and get a gestation age we could do one now. I really need you to focus on getting hydrated and taking it easy so if we have a VanByrne in there we take very good care of him."

Brian was smiling at Rachel and taking in the realization that Nate would want to be included in all this.

"On second thought why don't we go see Nate? We can discuss all the other things after we check on him. I know your anxious to get to him but the IV needs to stay in. You were very dehydrated and Nate would kick my ass if I didn't take care of you."

"Deal, now make me mobile so I can see him!"

Brian reached for the bag of fluids so he could move it to a portable stand and Rachel grabbed his arm.

"Can we hide it so Nate doesn't see it? Is there a smaller one or can we disconnect it for just a little bit? I don't want to worry him, he will be more concerned about me then getting better." "Rachel, we are not going to disconnect your fluids. I will explain to Nate, when he wakes up, that we are just giving you fluids. We can have the IV stand pushed close to the bed so he doesn't realize it's yours and not his. Deal?"

"Ok Doc, take me to Nate!" Rachel was worried about Nate but with Brian keeping it together, she knew Nate was going to be ok. Rachel was still very scared about her own test results but once she knew Nate was ok she would decide what she was going to tell him.

Brian changed Rachel's IV over to the portable stand and took her down the hall. Fortunately Rachel still had on her own clothes, if Nate was awake he wouldn't raise hell over Rachel's condition.

Since Nate and Rachel had become engaged, Nate was over the top protective of her. Nate had never been one to get serious in any relationship so that was a surprise to all of them. They all saw Nate's focus shift from training and work to Rachel then work. He had become obsessed with making sure he took care of Rachel, checking on her often, making sure she ate......he was completely in love.

"Ok Rachel, you go ahead and walk in and I will be right behind you with the IV. You can take the chair to the left of the bed that way the stand will be up by his head. Got it?"

"Got it." Rachel found herself replying to Brian in a breathy whisper. She didn't want to scare Nate, and if he was still sleeping she wasn't ready to wake him. As Rachel entered Nate's room she saw more bandages than she imagined and he was hooked up to all kinds of equipment.

"Brian please, is he going to be ok?" Rachel sobbed and sat in the chair as instructed. Tears flowed freely down her cheeks as she looked for any sign of her Nate in the bed next to her. Her Nate was strong, full of life and his fierce smile melted her heart but that isn't who was in the bed. He was pale and breathing heavy, like he hadn't slept in days. He was wrapped in bandages and had tubes everywhere, he looked like the shell of her Nate.

Brian saw the look on Rachel's face and slid a stool next to her. He grabbed her hand and gave it a reassuring squeeze as if to tell her he understood her fears.
"Rachel, Nate lost a lot of blood but he is getting some to replace it. His wound is going to heal and the results from the

bone scan should be back soon. I need you to relax, breathe and stop leaking the fluids we are trying desperately to put back in you." Brian was trying to get Rachel to smile but she could only nod her head without breaking her concentration on Nate. Rachel was silently praying that Nate was going to be ok.

"Brian, can I see you in the hall a moment?" Gale had returned from the radiology department and needed to update Brian.

"Sure Gale, Rachel I will be right outside that door. I need you to stay seated because you are still pretty weak, ok?"

Rachel nodded her response again, unable to form words. She needed to make sure that God heard her silent prayers, that was all that mattered now.

"Brian I have Nate's results back and they look good but he will need to see a specialist to be certain. He has a very small fracture on his c4 vertebrae but everything else looks good. We have him in a cervical collar now but if he heals well he could be out of it in four to six weeks. He is a lucky man, his guardian angel was working overtime this morning."

"That is amazing news Gale, thank you. I think I will hop out and let Granny know. I will just let Rachel know before I head out to the waiting area. Thanks again Gale."
Brian opened the door to Nate's room, Rachel was exactly as he had left her.

"Rachel I just spoke with Gale, Nate's tests are back and they are better than expected. He is going to be ok, he will need to take it easy for a few weeks but he should be fine."

Rachel looked away from Nate for the first time since coming into his room. Brian saw the happy tears begin as Rachel stood up and hugged him. Nate was going to be fine.

"Where the hell am I? Why is my head killing me? Brian you better let loose of my woman or I may just kick your ass!" Nate was awake and he was ready to raise hell to get up and out of the bed.

"Good afternoon little brother. I am going to run out and let Granny know you're awake. I think Rachel can fill you in on what happened and then I will be back in to give you an update."

Brian rushed out to the waiting area where Granny was still sitting. She was sipping something from a cup and resting her head on Mikey. The look of worry on her beautiful face would take a lifetime to forget but the news of Nate's condition would help.

"Granny, Nate just woke up and he is going to be ok. He has quite a few stitches, a very small fracture that should heal quickly and one monster headache. Rachel is with him now, she is doing well too. I have to go back in and talk to him then we will get you back there."
Granny stood and gave Brian the tightest hug she could and kissed his cheek.

"Thank you Brian! I knew Nate was going to be ok, I felt it in my bones. Now get back there so I don't have to wait any longer."
Brian nodded and headed back to Nate and Rachel.
When Brian reached Nate's door he heard what sounded like a

serious conversation between Nate and Rachel.

"Nate I am fine, really I am. I was sick so much that I just needed fluids, that's all. I am more concerned about you. How are you feeling?"

"Rachel I am fine, I have had worse. Granny can be a tough lady when you think you know better than she does." Nate chuckled and quickly winced at the pain in his neck.

"Nate there is something else I should tell you, need to tell you. Please promise me you won't overreact."

"Are you ok? What's really in the IV? I can take it Rachel, I love you."

"Ok, first……I love you so much and this may not be a thing but if it is, I am ok. Nate there is a pretty good chance……I might be pregnant." Rachel stood quickly and felt the room sway before quickly sitting back down.

A light tap on the door as it opened caught both Nate and Rachel's attention. Brian was back and felt this was a good point in their conversation to enter the room. Nate had not gotten a chance to respond before Brian was back at Rachel's side. She was pale and looked as though nausea was hitting her hard.

"I specifically told you to remain seated Rachel. You are no-where near ready to be on your feet. Since you have talked with Nate, let's get you into a bed so we can get that ultrasound. Nate before you say anything remember, I am the Doctor." Brian was going to get the ultrasound before he brought Granny back. Nate would be moved to a room upstairs soon and if Rachel wasn't with him, things were going to get difficult. Nate was as strong willed as he was strong so making him angry was a no win situation for the staff.

CHAPTER 6

"Mikey since we know Nate is going to be ok why don't you and Gabby head on back to the house. I won't be staying long, I really want Nate to rest. It's ok for you to head out too Paul, Nate is going to be fine. There is no reason for all of us to stay and keep him awake. Why don't you head on back to our house and I will cook dinner for everyone as soon as I get home."

"Granny it's been a really long day, why don't I grab some pizzas on the way home and we can all just relax. We will be back here tomorrow so we could all use the rest." Mikey was hesitant to leave without seeing Nate but Granny was right. Nate needed rest and if they all stayed, he wouldn't get it. Granny looked exhausted and having her work in the kitchen after the day's events seemed cruel.

"Pizza sounds perfect Mikey, thank you. Now you all head out and I will see you back at home in a bit. August you should head out with the kids, I am sorry you had to be involved in all this. I am sure you had plans for your vacation that didn't include babysitting me in the hospital waiting room. It was very sweet of you to stay with me but I release you of your gallant duties." Granny smiled at August, truly amazed that this man sat with her the entire day. Never once prying or offering any empty sentiments. He was her silent rock that provided her comfort without words.

"If it's ok with you, I can wait here until you see your grandson. I brought you here so the least I could do is to see to it that you make it home. Letty would never forgive me if I just left you here." August was hoping that last part would win Emma over. He loved just being near her and he felt needed, which was something new for him.

"If you are sure you don't mind. I guess I dismissed the kids not realizing how I was getting home. You are truly my hero right now, thank you."

Emma could feel herself blushing and prayed that it was only on the inside. Why this man had this crazy effect on her was confusing. Her heart hadn't raced like this since she first met Ben. She wasn't a silly teenager anymore, she was definitely not looking for anybody. There was just something about August that made her feel like she wanted to be protected.

"I will be seated right here until you are ready to leave, then we can ride back to the house together. Don't hurry, spend as much time as you need to with your grandson. I promise to be right here waiting." August returned to his seat as Brian came out to bring Granny back. She was very ready to see with her own eyes that Nate was ok. She also wanted to make sure Rachel was better. Rachel had earned a spot in her heart from the very first moment Granny met her.

"Brian I thought you were never coming out. How are they? Can

I see both Nate and Rachel? When can I take them home?"

"Granny I think you should hold off on any questions until you see them. Yes, you can see both Nate and Rachel. They are currently in the same room so you can see them without delay. Nate is a little cranky but he does have a headache. Rachel is doing much better but still getting fluids to help her regain her strength. They are both going to be ok but I know you won't believe it until you see it." Brian turned the handle on the door just as Granny pushed it open. She was a woman on a mission and nobody came between her and her kids.

"Oh my gosh Nate, how are you feeling? I have been worried sick out there with no news." Granny reached for Nate's hand and gave it a tender squeeze. She was beginning to get emotional just looking at Nate in that bed. He had a neck brace on, he was pale, there were still traces of blood on his gown and that had Granny scared.

"Granny I am fine, I just have a giant headache but other than that I feel ok. Rachel gave me a scare though." Nate looked over at Rachel causing Granny's eyes to follow.

"Rachel dear how are you feeling? Brian, do you know what's wrong with her yet? Do not keep it from me, she is almost my daughter and I have a right to know!" Granny was firing off like she had gotten in a good power nap. Her eyes were on Rachel but her words were directed at Brian.

"Granny, I am fine. In fact you are here at the right time." Rachel looked from Granny to Nate and he smiled in confirmation.

"Brian, we will take that ultrasound now please." Rachel smiled and climbed onto the bed next to Nate.

Brian nodded, left the room briefly and returned with a technician and a machine. It looked like they would find out together if the VanByrne family was going to need another place set at the family table.

"Rachel are you sure you want me here? Shouldn't tests be private? I know I am a force to be reckoned with but sweet girl I do not want to pry." Granny was trying to let them know she understood if they wanted her out of the room. She didn't want to know anything they weren't ready to tell her.

"Granny, Nate and I talked and we want you here whether it be good or bad. We are a family and there is nothing we wouldn't share with you."

Brian nodded to the technician to proceed as Rachel lifted her shirt exposing her very flat stomach. If there was a baby inside they were all here to witness his very first pictures.
When the technicians wand met the gel on Rachel's stomach a light pulsing sound filled the room. The screen was angled so Nate didn't have to turn his head to see it as all eyes were on the screen.
Nate held Rachel's hand and kissed her knuckles waiting to see what the future held. The wand began circling under Rachel's belly button when a thud began to pulse and the screen revealed a small dark pod. The only noise in the room came from the machine as everyone held their breath.

"Right here is what is causing all that commotion." Kate the technician said pointing to the screen and tapping buttons. "We have a little baby in here who looks to be about 7 weeks along. Can you see where I am pointing? He is moving around an awful lot in there but we definitely have a baby. Let me get a few more measurements and a couple more photos for......" Kate stopped speaking to look at the group. There were no words and not one single dry eye. It was so quiet Kate wasn't sure they were still in the room.

Rachel was the first to speak "Nate, we are going to be parents. It's really happening, we are going to have a little Nate running around. I have never been so happy and so scared in my life."

Nate was quiet as he stared at the screen, his grip on Rachel's hand remained. His eyes began to fill with tears as soon as Granny spoke.

"There is never a more sure sign that higher powers are in charge than what we have experienced today. Nathan you were saved by the grace of God today so that this blessing you both created will know your love. Life sends us in so many directions that we forget our purpose. Let today be a message to us all, our journey begins with each new sign. Before you give me your confused look Nathan, I want you to realize how today could have turned out. You have some healing to do but you will get through it. Rachel isn't sick she is blossoming into motherhood. True blessings and I couldn't be happier for you both. I may have sprouted some new gray hairs in the process but I will take them. I love you both so much and I can't wait to be chasing this little one around the kitchen."

Nate looked up to see Granny smile as tears cascaded down her smooth cheeks. He knew she meant every word of what she said. Growing up Nate went through a rough patch but Granny just loved him harder to get him through it. His child was going to know that same love. Granny had been their everything when they lost their parents and then their grandfather. Having her here, to be part of this journey, meant his child would love her too.

"Nate please say something, are you angry?" Rachel was starting to get nervous.

Nate moved his eyes to Rachel's and he saw the worry on her face.

"My silence isn't anger, it's awe. You are giving me something I never thought I needed until this very moment. I want this more than you could ever understand. We are having a child, our child. You Rachel are my world and now we get to share that world with the most perfect little being. We are going to be parents Rachel and nothing could make me happier." Nate kissed Rachel's hand he had been holding and whispered "I love you."

"Ok Kate, thank you for coming in. I think the new parents may need some privacy. Update Rachel's chart with everything and I will take it from here." Brian handed the pictures of the littlest VanByrne to Rachel and smiled at Granny as he gave her one too. "I think it's safe to say that Nate's room will need two beds. Rachel, we will just keep you for observation tonight. You guys need to promise to take it easy or I will call Granny." Brian chuckled out a laugh as Rachel began to blush.

"Granny, I will stay until they both get settled into their room. Then I need to get home for foot rub duty. I will call you with the room number so you can check on them but you should really get some rest." Brian knew Granny was getting tired but also knew she wouldn't leave on her own.

"I think I agree with you Brian, I am a little tired but worry will do that. Nate, Rachel I am so happy today was all good news. You kids get your rest now so you can come home." Granny hugged all three of them and kissed each one on the cheek. She paused on her way out the door to look at them again. This was what she had always wanted for her boys, a life full of love.

CHAPTER 7

When Emma came back into the waiting room her eyes found me immediately. I noticed they looked as though she had been crying and it made me want to hold her. I stood as she walked over to me, she appeared to be exhausted. I couldn't stop myself from taking her in my arms and hugging her. I don't know why but it felt right, like I had done it for years.......only I hadn't. She let me hold her, my arms wrapped around her like they belonged there and I loved it. I spoke first but couldn't bring myself to release her. Emma felt like home, I never wanted that feeling to escape me.

"Are you ok? Is everything ok?" I wasn't sure what to ask or how to ask it but I wanted to make everything better for her. I had to make everything better.

"Oh August, everything is better than I could have hoped for. Nate is going to be ok and Rachel, well she is carrying my great grandchild. Look, I have the babies first photo." Emma handed August the sonogram photo as a tear slowly made its way down her cheek.

August reached up and let his thumb gently capture the tear as he looked into her red rimmed eyes. Even with her puffy red eyes, Emma was intoxicating.

August found himself shutting out all that surrounded them, just so he wouldn't miss a second with her. He was afraid to blink and miss another tear or a shift in her lips. There was not one part of her he ever wanted to escape his memory.

"Emma that is wonderful news! Will you be staying longer to visit or should I get you home? I am fine with whatever you decide and I am not rushing you. I just want you to know, your carriage awaits when you are ready." August smiled as he spoke which was not something he was used to doing, smiling was a rare occurrence. It was rare, until Emma.

"You have been so sweet to wait here with me, then waiting for me. I appreciate your kindness and will be rewarding you with my culinary skills."

"I was hoping for a kiss but food is always a winner." August laughed nervously realizing he just made this awkward.

Emma could see that August regretted being so forward so she did the only thing she could to ease his tension. Emma stood on her toes and gave August the sweetest kiss before hooking his arm and asking for her carriage.

It must be the overwhelming joyful news I just received that made me do it. I just kissed a virtual stranger on the mouth in the hospital waiting room. He just looked so apologetic after almost asking for a kiss, I just couldn't let the moment go. The truth is, I am glad I did it. He is a handsome man, why would I not want to kiss him? I am actually quite shocked at how my body reacted to him after the little peck. I wasn't even sure those areas still worked after all this time. What just happened is proof positive that this old girl has all cylinders firing just fine. The electric pulse that shot from his lips to my........ummmm, areas, I had to hook his arm to stay upright. I know it's been a couple decades but is that even possible? They were just lips, warm, firm, gentle lips and I didn't even part mine. Now he is walking me to his SUV and I think my knees could fold. I need to get it together before he notices I am a heart racing, knee knocking mess. Thank the lord that was a short walk or I would have been a patient in the hospital we just left.

"Emma, are you ok to get in or would you like me to give you a hand? I know you must be exhausted after today and I don't mind." August was trying to get Emma to get into the passenger side of his vehicle but she was just .....out of it.

Shit! How long have I been standing at his SUV without climbing in the open door? I must be exhausted, there is no way I can be this affected. Jeez Emma use your legs and get in already!

"Thank you August, I am just taking in the events of today. It has been a long day but the news was just.........perfect." Emma climbed into the SUV and buckled herself in as August made his way to the driver side.

"Would you like to go straight home or do you need a coffee first? We aren't far from a great little coffee shop but I understand if you are ready to get home. You must want to share your great news with your family."

"I could really use a coffee but I do need to get home. Can we get one to go, I will buy since I held you prisoner all day. Then we can eat with the kids, only if you want to I mean. I hate that I have hijacked your day."

"Coffee then food sounds like a great ending but you are not buying. I enjoyed being with you today but I think our next outing should be a little less, sterile." August laughed until he realized what just came out of his mouth. Not only did he plan a another day with Emma but he insinuated it would be less than.......clean.

"Sorry, I think that may have come out a little differently than I would have liked. I just meant maybe the next time we enjoy each other's company it could be outside of the hospital environment, under better circumstances?" Where have my vocabulary skills gone? I deal with all sorts of people, celebs, wealthy socialites and even royalty but I spend one day with this woman, beautiful woman and I can't form any intelligent sentences!

"August I could not agree more and you did not need to explain yourself. I did raise three boys so I have that translation gene down." Emma gave August a genuine smile that came easily. He was very easy to be around, well until they touched lips, then everything went south, literally.....south.

Emma found herself getting lost, thinking about her life and the past.

Even though the ride home was not long my mind kept going to Ben, my Ben. That moment with August brought back feelings that were long forgotten and now the guilt was catching up to me.

Ben was my one and only for so many years. I loved him from the moment I saw him come into the restaurant that summer evening. I was there with my friends but when he entered I saw and heard nothing but him. He was handsome and had kind dark eyes that you just had to stare at. His one dimple when he smiled was intoxicating.

That's how we met, I was staring at him when he looked up at me. I think most girls would have been embarrassed but I just needed to look a little longer. He walked right up to our table and introduced himself to me. He was even more beautiful than I thought, handsome just couldn't describe it correctly. He asked me my name and that was all I needed, I knew from that moment I would marry him. Girls are like that, we can tell from hello if we love them and I did.

We spent every evening together that first summer and before the seasons changed I was wearing his ring. That beautifully handsome man asked me to marry him and I jumped at the chance to be his wife. My parents were not as eager to let me get married at 18 but Ben had no problem winning them over. When I married Ben I knew he would be my forever, my happily ever after. I didn't know how short forever was going to be. I was so broken when Ben died, I prayed for answers that never came. If it weren't for Evie's three beautiful little boys, my life would have been so different. They needed me so much but I needed them a whole lot more. Those handsome boys saved me.

August pulled up to Emma's house and quickly exited his vehicle. He was going to help Emma out of the car and inside the house. Just a few more moments to hold on to her wasn't too much to ask. There were several cars lining the street, a sure sign that Emma's family was waiting for her safe return.

CHAPTER 8

"Brian why are you so late? I made dinner for us but I will admit my feet are begging for that Brian magic." Sarah could see that Brian was distracted but she had no idea what had him so disconnected.

"I promised you that foot rub and I am a man of my word. Let's eat and I will fill you in on what happened while I give you the best foot rub you have ever had." Brian had planned on telling Sarah all about Nate but Rachel's news had to come from Rachel. If Sarah felt up to it he had plans on taking her to visit Nate and Rachel in the morning.

"Brian yours are the only foot rubs I have ever had, so if you plan on outdoing yourself let's hurry up and eat." Sarah grabbed Brian's hand and led him to the kitchen. The small bar area was set up with fresh chopped salad and warm baked bread. As Sarah pulled the lasagna from the oven Brian stepped behind her. He took the pan from her hands and placed it on the counter. He leaned forward and whispered softly into her ear "Every moment of every day, no matter what is happening around me, I know I am home right here." Brian captured Sarah's earlobe in his teeth then kissed her neck.

"You keep that up and we are skipping dinner." Sarah spun around in Brian's arms and began stroking the back of his neck, feeling his short hair with her finger tips.

"You look like you need to talk and I am here when you are ready. You know you can tell me anything Brian."

"It's just that Nate had an accident today while at work. He was taken to the hospital in bad shape." Brian paused as Sarah took a deep breath.

"He is going to be ok but I never want to see that look on Granny's face again. I have never seen her so scared. I don't know what I would do if I had to give her bad news. It was horrible to see her that way. There was a gentleman there with her, at the hospital. I don't think I have ever seen him before but they seemed..... close." Brian was not sure what had upset him more, Nate's injury or Granny finding comfort in a stranger.

"Ok, first question, Nate was hurt and taken to the hospital? What happened? How is Rachel handling all this?" Sarah was processing everything Brian had said but with all the information there were still questions.

"Second question, who was Granny with? How close were they? What did he look like?"

"Sarah I think your math skills are a little rusty. That was way more than two questions but let me clarify. Nate was injured by an airbag that fractured a vertebra in his neck but the biggest scare was the loss of blood from the laceration. It was a clean cut that closed up well but he did need a couple units of blood. He was unconscious for a little bit so he is staying at the hospital. He will need to be off work for a minimum of a few weeks but everything should heal well. Rachel has been sick so when she came to see Nate, she passed out. She too is staying the night but she should be fine after some fluids." Brian mentally checked off a list in his head, keeping track of all Sarah's questions.

"Granny arrived with an older gentleman who was over for lunch but I have no idea who he was. He seemed genuinely concerned about her but again, I do not know who he is."

"Wait, he was older?"

"Yes, do you know anything about him?"

"I stopped by Granny's this morning to grab a pan when Letty called, her brother in law was coming for a visit. He was grabbing a key from Granny because Letty had to leave for Georgia. It must have been him. Granny doesn't know him, well not before today anyway. I am sure you are reading too much into this, Granny had to have been upset maybe he was just helping her."

"I hope you're right but he looked to be pretty comfortable, comforting Granny. I am not sure I am going to be ok with that." Brian was not about to let some guy mess with Granny's heart. She was far more than someone's right now.

"Brian do you even hear yourself right now? Nate is in the hospital and you are ready to go all Thor on an older guy who was comfortable, comforting Granny." Sarah did air quotes as she repeated Brian's words and chuckled. If Nate is going to be ok there was no reason to get crazy. Brian was the oldest and always was the protector when it came to his family. He was definitely tired because this Brian was not himself right now. "Brian let's eat and then head upstairs for a nice warm bath, I will let you rub my feet." Sarah smiled with a soft pleading to her voice.

"You know I will never be able to tell you no, right? I think once these little ones arrive we are both in for a lot of yes's." Brian kissed Sarah's nose and took his seat at the bar. Dinner and a nice warm bath with Sarah sounded like the best medicine right now. He would talk with Granny tomorrow about the silver stranger and his intentions.

CHAPTER 9

"Thank you again for being with me today August, it was comforting having you there. I am sorry your first day was a complete disaster but it was still nice having you around." Granny was clearing the dishes from the table. Paul, Mikey and Gabby had taken off for the evening after making plans to visit Nate in the morning.

"Please stop thanking me for being there today. I am very grateful I was able to help even the tiny bit I did. It was nice to be needed, now let me help you with the cleanup. You have had quite a full day and I don't mind in the least." August was trying anything to spend just a little more time with Emma. He found himself thinking of things to say or do that would extend their visit.

"I am sorry, if you are tired I can just help clean up and then head over to Letty's. I hate keeping you up, I am sure you would like some rest as well."

"August I welcome your help but to be honest I have the house to myself for once and I am not sure I like it. We could watch something on television if you aren't ready to call it a night. I still have that pie if your in the mood for dessert."

"Pie sounds perfect and I could watch a little tv with you, if your sure it's ok."

"Let's get these dishes loaded up and I will get that pie cut. We can have it in the den while we watch something that isn't hospital related." Emma smiled as she began loading the dishwasher. Nervous she would be spending time alone with August but relieved the house was not empty. Mikey was spending lots of evenings away and soon would be out completely. Her once full house was beginning to empty.

August grabbed the pie plates and followed Emma to the den. It was a very large room with a television mounted above a sizable fireplace. There were 3 towers near the front window that appeared to be for a cat or cats to lay on. His office assistant Raya had gotten her kids a cat last year and had all sorts of things delivered to the office. It was pretty clear Emma had a cat. August had never had a pet growing up and did not get one as an adult, he didn't have time for pets with his crazy career demands.

"August let's sit on the sofa and you can take charge of the remote. I never know what to watch so you can surprise me." Emma smiled as she sat on the large sofa.
"Actually I don't really watch tv, we could just talk. Maybe just get to know one another." August was second guessing himself. What the hell am I doing? I sound like a teenager on a blind date. There has never been a point in my life where I felt so nervous around a beautiful woman, why now? Emma is just a woman, I have spoken to thousands of them. Why does it feel so different

being alone with her? I have this crazy urge to take her in my arms and protect her. Emma is not a frail woman who needs protecting, she is the exact opposite. She is a driven woman who screams independence but I can't help wanting to just shield her from the world. I have never been the kind of guy who wanted to protect any woman. I took care of Letty when my brother Arthur died but that was a different feeling all together. Emma brings out the caveman in me and I am not sure I am comfortable with this feeling.

"August? You didn't answer my question, are you feeling well? Should I let you head on back to Letty's? I didn't mean to keep you all day."

"I am sorry, I was thinking about….um, work. What was your question? I promise to be all ears now." August smiled but couldn't shake the feeling in his gut that told him, this was more, much more.

"I just wanted to turn on the music channel, is that ok? I will keep it low so we can chat." Emma was starting to feel warmth flood her face but it wasn't embarrassment.

"Music is perfect, anything will work. I listen to a wide variety so I will enjoy whatever you choose."

Emma clicked through the stations until she found the top 100 and smiled. She wasn't a metal head but she loved a lot of the current music. Not many of her friends enjoyed Sam Smith, The Jonas Brothers, Kane Brown and Ed Sheeran, so when she was alone they were in her ears.
As Emma glanced over slightly she saw August give a small

smirk as she stopped channel surfing. I guess he was ok with her choices.

"That is a great selection, I enjoy these artists too. Have you ever been to a concert for any of them? They are in New York frequently so I have been lucky enough to catch a few of them. I prefer to listen at home though, fewer distractions and a lot less people." Small talk, really? Emma has me sounding like a pubescent boy trying to make a good impression on the head cheerleader. Oh god now I am picturing her in a cheer uniform! I have got to get this under control!

"I have never been to a concert but I do agree with you about music at home. I have always loved the outdoors and music but never together." Oh my gracious, August is staring at me, like really seeing me! I am sure he is just trying to figure me out but it's been 72 years and I am still trying to figure me out. Good luck August, I go from hot mess to Queen B in nothing flat. August smiled and leaned back on the couch.

This conversation was going well, it's nice to just relax and enjoy some absolutely amazing pie and Emma. She is a refreshing change of pace for me, I think I like it.
I just wish I could figure out why my mind keeps telling me to make her mine. We only just met but I feel like I know her and what I don't know, I want to know.

"I am just going to run these plates to the kitchen, can I get you anything else? Coffee, another piece of pie?" Emma stood and stacked the plates in her hand as she turned to leave the room.
"I am fine, thank you but please allow me to help you. I can

carry the glasses and load the dishwasher. You have had a trying day, let me make your evening less stressful." Less stressful, really? That's the best I have? Why not just say, let me throw you on the couch and kiss you senseless? I have come to the sad conclusion, I have no game!

"Thank you, I will take you up on that offer."

Which offer, the one in my head? I liked that offer the most, kissing you senseless, yeah that's the one I want you to accept.

August smiled and picked up the glasses off the coffee table and followed Emma to the kitchen. He did as promised and loaded the dishwasher then headed back to the den. It was nearly 10:00 but he didn't want to go, not yet. He returned to his spot on the sofa and was shocked when Emma sat next to him. Emma put her head on his shoulder and released a sigh.
"It was so good of you today, with everything, to stay with me. I have been alone for a lot of years so it was hard to know I needed it. Thank you."

"You have got to stop thanking me, I could not leave you. I mean this in a very G rated way, but I had to stay near you. Emma there is something about you that draws me in and I can't stop it, I don't want to stop it. This is new to me and I may not know how to do it, handle this feeling I mean."

"August, that is sweet but you have had a long day. First your flight, then Rachel and lastly me. I am pretty sure this will all look different tomorrow..........."

Before Emma could finish her thought August crushed his lips to hers. It was urgent and hungry the way he devoured her words. No one had ever kissed her with such need and emotion before. Her Ben was always gentle and sweet when it came to romance. Those were the only kisses she ever knew but these breathless, hungry kisses were so much more. Her body was reacting in ways that had her starving for more. This was not normal behavior but right now she didn't want normal, she wanted more…… August, she wanted more August.

There was never any point in my life that I felt so out of control. Emma had me so crazy with need that I was afraid I was going to hurt her. When I pulled away for air, it was as if a force was pushing me back into her. I grabbed her with more force than I should have but a part of me was afraid she would leave. I had to stay connected to her lips and breathe her air, taste her tongue on mine. I needed this more than I needed to breathe, I knew I was never going to be able to stop this.

A loud commotion startled me back to life, as I opened my eyes I saw her face. Emma was laying beside me, hair everywhere and at peace in my arms. As I looked for the source of the noise I noticed not one but four kittens, at least I think they are kittens, curled up on my side. When I started to move I saw a fifth one cleaning its very hairy feet on the coffee table. Either I am dreaming I am in a Netflix series or Emma has a tribe of cats waiting on me to make a move. The sun was coming in the large window where two more, much larger cats, were lounging on the towers. I quickly looked at my watch and saw it was 7:30. I had spent the night on Emma's sofa and she was safely tucked in my arms. I have no idea how or what time we finally fell asleep but I really hope she was the first one to drift off. I don't think

I could look her in the face again if I was the one to fall asleep while kissing her. Kissing her, if I do nothing else in this life, kissing her is how I want it all to end.

"August what time is it? I am so sorry I fell asleep on you, I feel terrible."

Yes, she fell asleep first, thank you Jesus!

"Emma I can honestly say that that was the best nights sleep I have had in years. You need to stop apologizing to me, there will never be a time when you need to be sorry for anything."

Emma gave a sheepish grin and replied, "ok, I am not sorry I don't have time to make you breakfast. I need to get to the hospital to see Nate and Rachel and I am already running late."

"You run upstairs and get ready, I will make coffee and I will drive you to see the kids. Unless you would rather go alone?" As he spoke that last sentence his voice became softer. He wasn't ready to leave her just yet but he wasn't going to force himself into her day.

"Why don't you run and change while I shower. We can meet back here and go together. We can grab coffee on the way and grab something for the kids." Emma wasn't ready to let August leave her. Her lips still felt his burn and she couldn't help thinking she wanted to feel it again.

August stood and straightened his shirt before looking back at Emma.

"I will be back before you know it. Also, these are cats, right?"

August was pointing at the colony that surrounded him.

"They are and they are the sweetest little things, now go so we can go see my kids!"

CHAPTER 10

Mikey: *Guys we need a family meeting, like right now!*

Brian: *Why? What's going on?*

Mikey: *Granny had a sleepover, a sleepover with a stranger!*

Gabby: *Mike, I told you to not get involved in this. Granny is a big girl, she can handle her own life without you guys butting in!*

Nate: *What the hell is going on? You guys better not have a family meeting without me!*

Brian: *Mikey are you sure about this? That is not sounding like our Granny at all.*

Mikey: *I saw it with my own two eyes this morning! What happened to the whole stranger danger shit?*

Nate: *If you are messing with me I will kick your ass! Just because I am a little under the weather doesn't mean you're safe!*

Brian: *You are way more than under the weather Nate and you are not kicking anyone's ass. We need to talk to Granny about this before we get crazy.*

Mikey: *Guys, I can't unsee it, it is burned into my retina's, my* *retina's! This is going to have a long term effect on me! I may need therapy!*

Sarah: *Stop this, all of you! I will talk to Granny, none of you will say anything! A woman needs another woman to talk to about this stuff, not you Neanderthals! Now get to work, except you Nate. You need to rest and get better. Gabby, you are invited to join me. You guys........stay away!*

Granny: *Is now a good time to remind Mikey that family chat includes me? Gabby and Sarah I would love a girls get together soon but you boys are in big trouble! I did nothing except fall asleep on the sofa with a new friend because we were exhausted. Nate I will be there soon to visit you with August, my new friend. Love you all.*

Well shit! How did I pick the wrong group for the text? Now Granny knows I saw them, both of them. Cuddling on the couch like teenagers on movie night. I am not letting this go, I need to talk to the guys in private. Why the hell is she so easily caught up in this guys spell?

"Mike we need to go visit Nate before your first patient is scheduled. Can we head over now?" Gabby was dressed and ready to head out when Mike showed up at her front door in a panic this morning.

"I think I will wait until lunch to head over there. I think Granny is going to go this morning anyway and I am not sure I am ready to face her yet." Mike was not ready to run into Granny just yet, he needed to do some research first.

"Gabby if you don't mind staying until lunch we can go over to visit Rachel and Nate together. I need to talk to Nate and Brian about *the incident* anyway. I just don't understand what was going through Granny's head. She let a stranger sleep over and it wasn't all pure and innocent. They were spooning and Granny was the little spoon! The little spoon Gabby! That means her friends little morning soldier was knocking on Granny's back door!!" Mike was rubbing his temples and leaning on the kitchen counter in Gabby's very small kitchen.

"Mike, it's fine, it's all fine. Nate and Rachel are going to be ok. Granny has been alone for a lot of years. I think it is wonderful she is opening up her world to a new person. I know you don't feel that way but Letty would never allow anyone to hurt Granny and it's her brother in law. Just don't get crazy with this and make Granny upset, ok?"

Mike nodded his head but wasn't exactly sure what he was going to do.

As Mike headed out the door, ready to get to his office, he could not get the picture of Granny out of his head. She was so blissful and relaxed, like she had done this for years. Only she hadn't done this, ever!

Not one single time growing up had any man ever gotten that close to her. There were guests that would come and stay throughout the years at the B&B who tried to show interest but Granny would not have it. The one thing that Mikey always knew growing up was that he and his brothers were the only men she ever wanted in her life.

They were all settling into their lives now, as adults. Was that it? Granny was replacing them with this new guy, because they

were all moving on with their lives and families.
Was she feeling forgotten? Maybe she was feeling less needed now. There was no question now, he needed to talk to his brothers. He would text Brian to meet up with him at lunch to visit Nate. They would figure this out before it was too late.

Now Mikey just needed to get through his morning patients without losing his shit.

When Mikey arrived at his office he found Paul waiting on the steps.

"Mikey can we talk for a few minutes? I think I need to talk to someone and Gabby suggested that maybe you could help me out. If not I understand." Paul looked like he hadn't slept at all since yesterday.

"I have time Paul, come on in. Can I get you a coffee? I know I could use one." Mikey placed the pod in the coffee maker and sat down on the small couch. Paul took the chair across from him and looked haunted as he began to speak.

"When I was in the Army we had a lot of missions over there, you know, over seas. Some of them not nearly as successful as others. We lost some good soldiers, you know. Everything happened so fast, one minute your joking about holding your liquor and before you know it….your holding someone's leg together with your bare hands." Paul took in a long breath and folded his hands together around his neck.

"When Nate got hurt, when the bag deployed? It brought out a lot of those memories, ones I had buried. I can't relive those Mikey, I can't come back from that. I froze when Nate got hurt, the blood, it made me feel helpless. I can't do what I do, what I love and feel helpless. I know this whole mental shit isn't your job but it feels better getting it out. I felt better when I talked to Gabby yesterday so I thought maybe, you know?"

Mikey knew Paul served several tours over seas and saw quite a few battles. Never had it crossed his mind what something like that could do to someone. Paul was closer to Brian's age but everyone in this small little town knew each other. What Paul was dealing with sounded like PTSD but he needed to get help. Talking to a professional was what Paul needed if he was going to get through this.

"Paul you know you can talk to me anytime about anything but I think maybe you can get some help from a support group. There are a lot of people who come back and have a tough time. Some have triggers, like what I think happened with you. I am not a psychologist but I truly believe you may benefit by talking to one." Mikey had become pretty familiar with most doctors in the area. There were a few he would suggest but Paul could really benefit from a support group. If Paul resisted Mikey would direct him to a group and keep trying to get him to see a doctor.

"Mikey I have known you for a long time but I am not sure about a doctor. I mean, they can't take away what I have seen, what I saw while serving. Talking helps, maybe talking would be a good place to start but I am going to be honest, I am skeptical. I have to try something because doing nothing may not end well." Pauls voice became a whisper as he finished talking. Mikey was not letting Paul leave without agreeing to a support group. Sometimes you have to work at making your mind stronger than your emotions and this was definitely one of those times.

Making my mind stronger than my emotions? How the hell did I get so smart and so dumb at the same time? Maybe I should take my own advice and get my emotions in check. Granny will kick my ass if I let my emotions control my actions, butting into her personal life.

CHAPTER 11

"August you are the best, this coffee is amazing but you didn't need to buy scones too. My butt doesn't need pastry, it needs coffee but the kids will appreciate them. Thank you for being so…..amazing, when you didn't have to be." Emma was trying to act like she was unaffected by August and the pretty steamy kisses they shared last night. Problem was, she was very affected and it made a simple conversation feel very difficult. August was not someone that Emma needed to be attracted to. That's what this was, right? Attraction? It felt way more intense than that but how do you label what was going on in her head and every other region of her body? August was causing all kinds of reactions, some of which hadn't been felt in over 20 years. How is that even possible?

"Emma I really enjoy your company and at some point we should talk about last night. I don't want this to get awkward, we are consenting adults and quite frankly I really enjoyed it. All of it, including waking up covered in cats, holding you while you slept. It was honestly one of the best nights sleep I have had in a very long time." August was trying to steal glances at Emma as he drove but each glance made him not want to turn away.

He had hoped to catch her reaction to his honesty, maybe she would return the exact same feelings.

"August, last night was........very unexpected. It was something I had never thought I would be doing at my age but I ....I really enjoyed it, all of it. This is hard for me to admit, having only ever kissed one man until last night. I know he has been gone for a lot of years but when I lost him, I lost a part of me. Spending time with you, kissing you, it woke that part of me that I thought I had lost. I don't want you to think that I am stuck in the past but it is hard for me to move forward. I loved Ben, that was his name, for more years than I have been without him. When you kissed me with such passion, I couldn't pull away. I wanted those kisses as much as you did and you are right, we are consenting adults. What I am trying to say is...... I consent August, I consent to more." Emma's voice became soft as she finished speaking. August reached for her hand and she let him gently caress her palm.

How in the hell did I get so lucky? I dropped everything in New York to get away from the madness that had become my life and I meet the most intriguing woman the first hour I am here. Having Letty off in Georgia was a blessing in disguise. I am happy she is welcoming her granddaughter into the world but happier that it left me with Emma.

Does that make me an asshole?

I should be overjoyed that my brother had a granddaughter entering the world even if he wasn't here to enjoy it. I would of course take over for him and spoil that child like she were mine but my focus, right now, is this amazing woman beside me. Is it wrong that I want to fill the void left by her husband? I want to hold this woman and give her more, much more and I don't think two weeks will be enough. I have a life in New York, I have people who depend on me.

"Emma I know you have a family that needs you right now. I want you to know I respect that but I want more time with you. I want to take you out, I want to feel your lips on mine again and I want to hold you. I want you to take whatever time you need for your family but if you have any time to spare I want it, all of it. I know your heart isn't yours to give and I appreciate your honesty but I am here and I am yours when you are ready." I am here and I mean every word but I am not sure if what I have to offer is enough. Enough for her to move forward, enough for us to explore if there even is an us.

"August you are such a kind man and I can tell you mean every word. Let's go see my kids and take them the treats you bought. If we soften them up maybe it won't be so terrifying when we have to face the jury. We are in for a lot of cross examination when we get back home......I mean, back to my house." These boys have been my whole world, now that they are beginning new chapters in their lives is it so wrong that I am finding my place without them? Mikey was so little when we became our little family, maybe that is why he is so protective. These boys need to understand that I can guard my own heart if I need too, right?

"Emma, we are here. Would you like me to wait in the lobby while you visit the kids? I don't mind if you need some alone time with them, I can work on my emails while you visit."

"Thank you August but I think I am safer if you come with me. I think I will avoid a multitude of questions if you are there. Do you mind coming with me?"

"I will be anywhere you want me to be. Let's get these pastries up to those kids and throw out a small prayer that it helps us avoid an inquisition" August chuckled as he took Emma's arm and they made their way to the elevator. Although he wanted Emma to believe that he felt the VanByrne boys were harmless, part of him was certain they could be very protective when it came to Emma.

Just as they exited the elevator August's phone began to vibrate in his pocket.

Damn it, who could possibly need to speak to me at this early hour? I do not need any distractions when my time with Emma is ticking away. I get 14 days off, well 13 now and I need to take valuable minutes to coddle some ad exec who is on a time crunch.

"I am sorry Emma, do you mind if I take this call? I promise to be quick since I don't recognize the number, then I am all yours."

"August please take your call, I can handle the kids just fine. If it gets to be too much I will just tell them we eloped. That should silence them until you finish up." Emma smiled then headed to Nate and Rachel's room. Once she reached the door she turned to see August staring at her as he spoke into his phone.

"August here, what can I help you with?"

"August, it's Letty. I am using the hospital phone because I can't get a signal in this hospital. I wanted to check on you and make sure you got in the house ok. I am sorry I wasn't there but babies come on their own time."

"Letty, is everything ok with the baby? How is little Amy doing? Have they chosen a name yet? Emma will ask of course so I should get those details for her."

"What do you mean Emma will ask? Are you with her? You sound funny, is there something I should know?"

"Focus! Name? Mother and baby doing well? Do they need anything? I can have it there in the hour just name it."

"Always the hero. Mother and baby are doing very well actually considering. Amy has chosen the name Rose Jewel and she was 8lbs. even and 20 inches long. We need to talk when you have some time later tonight. I am concerned about Amy. I think things are not going well at home and I am hoping I can bring them back home with me. I need to talk to her some more without stressing her out but I think it will be for the best. Please keep that last part to yourself and I will call you tonight if that's ok?"

"Say the word and I will have tickets waiting for you all. If I need to come get you, I can do that too."

"I know and thank you but I need to speak with Amy. I think she is keeping me out of it for a reason. I will get to the bottom of it and update you later. Give my love to Emma and thank you August, for being you. Gotta go, Amy is due back in her room any minute and she would give me hell for worrying you."

Nothing about that call sounded good except for Rose Jewel of course. Amy chose a beautiful name, my mothers name, for her child. Arthur would be so proud, I can just picture him running the halls handing out bubble gum cigars.

CHAPTER 12

"Brian you have three patients this morning so can we go see Nate and Rachel after the last one? Take an early lunch?" Sarah was still working in the file room at Brian's office but it wouldn't be long before she would need to stay off her feet more. Brian wanted her to rest and stay home but Sarah wanted to stay as active as her body would allow.

"Of course we can. Why don't you stay at the reception desk until we take off. You do not need to be on your feet. This way we can leave as soon as the last patient checks out." Brian bent down and kissed Sarah softly on the lips as he sat her in the desk chair. When he was sweet like this Sarah could not bring herself to argue. Brian was tender and doting when it came to Sarah and their babies, always putting them first.

As Sarah began getting familiar with the reception desk she noticed the door to the office open. She watched as a beautiful woman entered and looked around. This could be an early patient arrival or a pharmaceutical rep, either way Sarah was ready to greet her.

"Can I help you? Do you have an appointment with Dr. Van-Byrne?" Sarah was seated behind the desk when the woman approached and flashed her a perfect smile. This had to be a sales rep, she was too primped to be a patient.

"No appointment dear but I am certain Brian will see me. Tell him his wife is here, he will make time for me." The woman's smile seemed far less beautiful the moment she said wife. This was Brian's ex-wife and she was enjoying this far too much.

"You must be Kim, Brian's EX-wife. Please have a seat and I will let Brian know you are here." Sarah stood and turned to get Brian when she heard Kim comment on her weight.
Did she not see the maternity smock?

Sarah tapped on Brian's office door and gently pushed it open. Brian was reading a file and looking at his computer screen. His face showed some concern but when his eyes met Sarah's his smile soften his brow.

"I think I like seeing you in my office a lot more than that file room. Come here and let me get you off your feet." Brian stood and held out his arms for Sarah to come to him.

"As inviting as that sounds, you have an unscheduled visitor in the waiting area and she isn't very nice." Sarah smiled but it wasn't a genuine smile. The beautiful woman in the waiting area was vile and her venom was a sure sign this was not going to be a pleasant visit.
Brian gave Sarah a look of confusion but followed her out to the seating area. Sitting in one of his waiting room chairs was a very primped and polished ex wife. Kim looked bored and agitated but when she saw Brian her demeanor changed. Kim stood and rushed to embrace Brian like she was his long lost love. Brian didn't return the hug, he just looked at Sarah in complete shock.

When enough time had passed Brian removed Kim's hands from his body and stepped back. The look on Kim's face told Brian that she was not happy about his distance. He didn't care but he didn't need for Sarah to be put through stress in her condition either. Kim had made her choice when they divorced and it was the best thing that could have happened. Brian found Sarah again, he was having the children he had always wanted and he was madly in love. Sarah was his oxygen, his strength behind the beating of his own heart. Sarah was always his ever after, happily ever after.

"Kim, why are you here? We settled everything months ago, shouldn't you be in LA by now? I am sure your surgeon is missing you." Brian couldn't help himself, he had lost all feeling he had for Kim so everything he said sounded cold and distant.

"Brian that is not fair, I have always loved you. We hit a bump in the road but love doesn't just stop when things get tough. Let's go to lunch and talk, I have missed you."

"What the hell…." Brian began to speak when he felt Sarah grab his hand and squeeze.

"I am sorry, Kim was it? Brian will not be taking you to lunch nor will he be free for dinner. You can take your gold digging ass back to your hotel or livery stable and join a dating site. My husband and I have no time for you or your games while we shop for our babies. You see Brian and I are having triplets and all our spare time is being devoted to us and our growing family. I am assuming you remember how you got here so please see your way back out!" Sarah was calm but direct as she spoke, not once looking away from Kim's shocked face.

"Brian, what is she talking about? We have only been divorced a few months, how did this all happen? Were you cheating on me?" Kim was letting her anger boil into a shouting rage as she glared at Sarah. Brian held Sarah to him as he chuckled in Kim's direction. The pride he felt in Sarah for standing up to Kim was overwhelming.

"The adultery was your thing Kim, not mine but thank you. If you weren't the disgusting, evil woman you were I would never have found my one true love. Sarah and my children will be all I ever need in life so please see yourself out before I call security. My wife doesn't need your toxic garbage and quite frankly I won't allow it."

Brian bent down and kissed Sarah's head as he pulled her tight against him. There was only one woman for him and he knew that the very first summer he met Sarah.

"I will leave but understand that once I go out that door Brian, we are through. You won't be able to run back to me when that litter she is carrying gets too much for you. Don't get me started on stretch marks or saggy skin, you may as well say goodbye to sex for the rest of your life. Have a nice life and I don't mean that!"

Kim left the office but made sure to slam the door on her way out. She was always selfish and vile to others but Brian had hoped she would soften up when they married, she didn't and still hadn't.

"Sarah come back to my office for a minute, we have some time before any patients arrive. I want to hold you and revel in your badassery. You are the strongest most amazing woman I know and I am so lucky I get to keep you." Brian led Sarah back to his office and sat her on his desk. He pulled off her shoes and began massaging her very swollen feet. As mad as Sarah was at the evil bitch's visit she was enjoying Brian's attention to her. He always put her first and this foot rub was one of his many talents. Some of the things Kim said hurt but she was just saying them to be mean.

"You know Brian she was right. I will be covered in stretch marks and my skin will sag. I am ok with the changes that giving life makes to my body but will you still feel this way? When everything doesn't fall back in place, will you still love every inch of me?" Sarah was speaking as if she entered a dream state. She spoke as though she could fall asleep at any moment but the pain in her voice was still noticeable.

"Sara Nichole VanByrne! I have loved you since the very first summer you stayed at your Grans house. I was lost when you were gone, you saw where heartbreak led me. It wasn't pretty! There will never be a moment I look at you and not see the beautiful, loving, amazing woman you are. I want to kiss every wrinkle and caress every crazy white hair that ever sprouts out of your beautiful head. If bringing our babies into this world gives you are roadmap of stretch marks, I promise to kiss each one goodnight, every night, for the rest of our lives. You Sarah, can never be rid of me, I need you to breathe, I will always need you to breathe." Brian continued to rub Sarah's feet as he kissed her leg softly. Her soft moans in response were all he needed to hear. He and Sarah were lifers, they were always meant to be.

"Brian, you may have to stop or put a cot in here. I can't seem to keep my eyes open when you talk all sweet to me and give me these amazing massages." Sarah smiled as Brian started to put her shoes back on her feet. He just needed to get through a couple patients, then the afternoon was theirs to wash away the filth that Kim left in her wake.

CHAPTER 13

"Nate honey, Granny is here to make it all better. I have coffee for you and caffeine free tea for Rachel. We also have some wonderful pastries for you both, now tell me how you are feeling."

"I need coffee and sugary pastries please and thank you." Rachel was slowly pulling herself off Nate's chest, still half asleep. He was insistent that Rachel sleep in his bed so he could hold her as she slept. The pain in his neck was tolerable but holding Rachel and feeling her in his arms was all he needed to get through this.

"No coffee Rachel unless it's decaf. We talked about your caffeine addiction last night and how it isn't good for the baby. We are in this together so I will pass on the coffee too but I hope you brought several pastries because I am starving." Nate was in good spirits and caressing Rachel's hair as he spoke to Granny. He and Rachel spent the night discussing the wedding plans, baby plans and what Nate's future will look like. With a baby coming Nate wasn't sure that his job was the best choice for his health or his family.

"Well my sweet boy, it's a a good thing I grabbed two cups of tea. Now you can have a hot drink and this bag of scones August bought you both. I will keep the coffee so you are not tempted." Granny placed the bag and cups of tea on the bedside tray and placed her hand on Nate's cheek.

"Nathan David, you are the strongest man I know but in my heart you are still my sweet little boy. You gave me quite the scare and I prayed so hard that you would be ok but this has aged me. I don't know if I could take another scare like that one. You have a beautiful baby on the way and a gorgeous fiancé you need to think about now. I know you love your job but maybe you could scale back on the super human stuff?"

"Granny, Rachel and I talked quite a bit last night and I think maybe it's time to put my degree to use. I am not saying I am done with the whole first responder thing but you are right. Nothing in life is more important than Rachel or our children, before you ask, we plan on more than one child in our future." Nate kissed Rachel's hand that had been resting on his chest and winked at Granny.

"Since we are on the subject of life, can I ask about you and August? Nate and I heard about your evening and were curious as to what is going on. I thought he mentioned to me that he was Letty's brother in law. I am so grateful that he was there, he saved me yesterday. Have you known him long? Is there something we should know about?" Rachel knew Nate wanted these details but he would not be so gentle in his questioning. If she got this out of the way while Granny was alone maybe it wouldn't be so awkward for any of them.

Emma's mind immediately went to the first kiss she and August shared and how her lips burned when she thought about it. How firmly he held her and the need she saw in his eyes. He was someone she didn't realize she needed in her life but last night made her and her body very aware of her needs. Maybe it was the events of the day that made her so needy. Maybe she was reading more into what happened but she knew she wanted it to happen again.

"Granny? Are you ok? I am sorry if that was too personal, I just thought maybe you would like to talk about it. We don't have to talk about it if you would rather not." Rachel was sitting up now as Nate held her close.

"Oh my goodness kids. Yesterday was a nightmare and August was good enough to bring me here and stay with me all day out of the kindness of his own heart. He brought me home after we knew you both were going to be ok. We had pizza and pie then fell asleep on the sofa in the den. You will be delighted to know that the little kittens loved him and slept on him all night. They are amazing judges of character so you have nothing to worry about. He is the brother of Letty's husband, rest his soul, and is just here for the next two weeks. I will be a great friend, in Letty's absence, show him around town and cook for him, nothing more. I love that you are all concerned for me, given your current state, but I am fine. When Letty returns he will be spending time with her, then he will head back to his life in New York. He is harmless and really doesn't have an evil bone in his body." Granny did her best to make the kids believe what she was saying even though her heart was hoping for more.

"Good, I don't want to kick an old guys ass but I will if I have too." Nate was chuckling when he spoke but his eyes showed a serious concern.

Granny was everything to these boys. She was the glue that held them all together. Each of them would stop at nothing to protect her from anything that jeopardized her happiness.

"Nate it isn't like we eloped, stop being so grumpy. You are going to be going home before you know it and you will get to know August better. He is really a nice man with good intentions, trust me." Because Granny was so focused on Nate she missed August coming to the doorway.

Oh my god, it must be bad!
Emma just told these kids we eloped! Do I play along and let them think we are married? Even in that hospital bed, Nate looks like he could do some serious damage. If Emma wants to pretend to be married I guess I am all in.

"Letty sends you her best dear, I trust your visit is going well? When you are done we will need to head over to Letty's so I can grab my things but please take your time. We have the rest of our lives to get everything together." August pulled Emma to his side and kissed her cheek.
That's what married people do, right? Why is everyone staring at me? I am certain I heard Emma tell them we eloped. Why do I feel like I read this room all wrong?

"I was just telling the kids how we are just spending time together until Letty returns. Why do you need your things? Are you leaving earlier than planned? Oh dear is Letty ok?" Emma began to panic but quickly realized the confusion on August's face meant a serious misunderstanding.
"August can we slip out to the hall for a second? I need to talk

with you about something and the kids need to eat." Emma quickly ushered August to the hall out of earshot.

"Emma I think I missed something here. I thought I heard you tell the kids we eloped. I figured it was best to play along but now I think I may have created a bigger problem." August was rubbing his neck and looking nervously back in the direction of the room they just left.

Emma busted into a full body shaking laugh as she reached for August's free hand. The whole time August was meeting Nate for the first time he was pretending to be her husband. Now she had to find a way to undo this fiasco before Nate alerted the rest of the family. As funny as this situation was, it wasn't fair to August to be subjected to that.

"Oh this is too funny not to enjoy but I think you caught part of the conversation and it is definitely my fault. I should have never told you I was going to tell the kids we eloped if they gave me any trouble. This whole mix up is on me but you have to admit it is a little funny." Emma's smile was infectious which made August smile and shake his head.

This woman has me all tied up in knots. How did a man like me become this giant mess? For a few moments I was enjoying the thought that Emma was my wife. I felt at home when I pulled her in and kissed her just minutes ago. I could do it again but I am guessing that is not going to help us explain what just happened.

"We better go back in there and fix this Emma. Do you think they will be upset or find the humor in this?"

"I think they will definitely find this funny but you better leave the explaining to me." Emma walked with August back into the room that Rachel and Nate shared. As they entered the room Rachel was the first to speak.

"Before Nate tries to get out of this bed, please tell me you guys are not married. Even if you are please tell me you're not. I don't think I can hold Nate down if he tries to kill August."

"There is no way I would get married without my boys. I was playing a little joke to get even for the group text and poor August got pulled into it. I promise I am not married and my friendship with August is as pure as the driven snow. Now tell us how you both feel. When will they let Nate head home and what are his restrictions?"

CHAPTER 14

"What do you mean Granny pretended to be married? Nate what meds do they have you taking?" Brian and Sarah no sooner made it into Nate's room when they received the news. After the morning they had with Brian's ex-wife this was beginning to feel like a bad dream.

"Look, Granny was here this morning with that guy but swears they are just friends. She says she was just going to play a joke on us because of that text Mikey sent but I saw the way that August guy looked at her. Dude, I think we need to watch him close." Nate was trying hard to be optimistic but Granny was Granny and no one was going to hurt her, no one.

Brian took in everything Nate had to say and tried to rational-ize it. Granny has always maintained a level head in everything. She would never let herself get into any questionable situ-ations. Her whole life was dedicated to her boys and her giving nature. Granny always made sure to give back and genuinely cared for others first. This scenario Nate was sharing was com-pletely out of character.

"You need to take it easy, both you and Rachel. Brian and I will look into this August guy and take it from here. I will have plenty of time on my hands now that Brian is hovering over me and these babies like a mother hen. I swear if my feet get any bigger I will need to represent the barefoot and pregnant stereotype until their arrival." Sarah was rubbing her belly as she spoke, looking adoringly at Brian the whole time.

"Speaking of babies, Nate and I are expecting our own little bundle. It was a complete shock and definitely not planned but I am so happy. Our babies will grow up together Sarah, can you believe it?" Rachel was much more alert today, glowing with joy knowing she and Nate were going to have a baby.

"That is amazing news, I will save you my maternity clothes since I am growing out of them so fast. Spandex is life, well that and these super stretchy maxi dresses. I have found comfort far outweighs fashion these days but it is so exciting." Sarah sat down in the chair next to Brian and took a deep breath. These babies were battling for position in their very confined space making Sarah constantly look for relief.

Movement in the doorway drew everyone's attention as Gabby and Mikey walked in to the room. Mikey was showing a look of concern as he entered the room but Nate knew it wasn't concern about him.
Mikey had been so little when they lost their parents and then their grandfather. Granny was every bit a mother in Mikey's eyes and this new guy was making Mikey more agitated than the rest of them.

"Mikey, cool you're here too. We were just discussing my visit from Granny this morning. She was in good spirits but she did have a friend with her, they brought us food." Nate was smiling, hoping to get Mikey to relax a bit but the scowl he was met with told him.....plan fail.

"Look guys, I am not a fan of this new guy and I certainly don't think Granny needs anyone to get all cozy with her, especially at her age. Seriously guys, this is not cool. I mean what do we really know about this guy?" Mikey was pleading his case, hoping to get everyone on board.

"According to photographer weekly, this man is top five in the country for his photography skills. He also has a very impressive net worth based on this quick internet search. Did you know he is responsible for creating three very large food kitchens for the less fortunate? His client history is full of pretty impressive names, like really impressive. I definitely don't think he is after money, so maybe his intentions are pure." Rachel was scrolling through her phone reading off accomplishments to the group. August had quite the reputation in New York for giving to charity and being surrounded by beautiful models but had never been seen out with anyone. There were rumors that he had a secret life and a wife in another state but it seemed those all pointed back to Letty.

"He seems to be a successful, stand up guy according to everything I am reading. Trust me, the reporter in me can sniff out any bullshit and I don't smell anything here. Except coffee, I smell coffee! Which one of you is drinking coffee in here? I am a starving girl here, please take pity on me." Rachel was realizing her sense of smell was taking on superpowers and her need for coffee was fueling them.

"So he is a famous photographer in New York but he is Letty's brother in law too?" Sarah was putting all the information together as she spoke. "Mikey why are you so skeptical of him?"

"What kind of guy takes a woman to the hospital, then stays attached to her hip all day then stays the night? Is that the kind of guy we want Granny associated with?" Mikey was pleading his case to his brothers when all three girls answered in unison.

"Yes!"

"It's sounds so sweet to have a man want to protect us and comfort us when we need it. I think he was sweet to want to take care of Granny when she was so upset. Maybe they really did just fall asleep after a long day. You guys need to look at this rationally and not like cavemen. I think you guys need to give Granny your support and not your resistance on this. If it goes south or goes really good don't you want to be there for her? Let her come to you if she needs it, not telling her what she needs." Sarah was going to support Granny on this and these boys needed to realize she was a grown woman and strong enough to guard her own heart just fine.

CHAPTER 15

August dropped me off at home after we left the hospital, Letty needed him to run a couple errands. He was very clear when he left, that he had made plans for us for a late lunch. This man had been by my side since he arrived in town but he had time to make lunch plans? I was more than happy to let him take me to lunch, I enjoyed his company. No, I loved his company and I was hoping Letty took her time coming back. I wasn't quite sure I wanted to share him just yet. I am not sure what was happening between us but time with August made me feel…….all the feels, everywhere my body allowed.

The light tap on the front door pulled my attention away from my thoughts. It was still a little early so I wasn't sure who would be coming over. When I reached the door and peered out I saw a young man in a suit. There are very few causes for suits in this town, weddings and funerals were just about all the warranted this attire. I was prepared to point to the "no soliciting" sign next to the door once I opened it but this young man addressed me by name.

"I have a car waiting and I was given strict instruction not to share our destination. You may want to grab a sweater but please don't tell him I told you that." The young man followed up his instruction with a soft smile.

"Can I ask who sent you? I don't make a habit of climbing into strangers cars and I prefer not to start today." Emma smiled and reached for a sweater in the front closet as she stepped out onto the front porch.

"I understand ma'am, I was hired by a Mr. Wander, August Wander? Does that provide you any reassurance or should I make a call?"

"I should have figured he would do something like this. Can you tell me if I am dressed appropriately or if I should pretty myself up with a dress or heels?"

"Without giving you any details, you look perfect for your date. No changes would be required to enjoy your outing." The young man smiled and winked at Emma as he gestured toward the awaiting car. A very expensive, very large, shiny new car.
The ride was familiar but where would August be taking her for a date? He wasn't from here, does he know where he is sending her? The scenery was so beautiful out this way. The upward climb of the car was familiar but the left turn at the large oak tree solidified her suspicion. He was taking her to the hot spring overlook. It had been decades since she had been up here but the view she remembered was breathtaking.
Would they be hiking? Silently thanking herself for wearing leggings and sneakers, Emma was ready for anything this date brought.

"We should be there shortly, I have been instructed to keep you in the car until your date arrives, in the event we are early." The young man smiled politely and watched Emma from his rear view mirror.

Emma nodded her head and gazed out the window at the beautiful scenery. Some of the trees had grown and the foliage was thicker but the sky and the view was all still the same.
Ben was sweet when he brought her here for the first time. They were young, it was fall and they wanted to soak in the hot spring. They had been dating for three months when he brought her here as a surprise. They had talked and kissed for hours before Ben pulled the ring from his trunks and asked her for forever. It was a beautiful memory to hold on to. They managed to come back a few times over the years but after their daughter was born they stopped coming.

"Emma, are you ready for an adventure?" August asked as he held out his hand to help her from the car.
Once Emma exited the car, it slowly pulled away and disappeared in the distance. Emma was alone in the woods with August and the afternoon was fading. August held Emma's hand as they walked to the overlook, taking in the view of the small town below. The aging wood bench was covered with initials of all the young lovers who took in this same view. It was a reminder of all the young hearts that had been here over the years and all the promises made. It was both heartwarming and heartbreaking at the same time.

Emma smiled at August and waited for him to lead her, she would definitely follow him.......anywhere.

"I hope this is ok, I found this spot years ago after Arthur died.

It gave me peace and I wanted to share it with you, share a little bit of me with you."

"This place holds memories for me as well, sweet ones but I would love to have new memories to keep with me. It's been a lot of years since I have been up here but everything still looks the same. I love that you brought me here, it's beautiful. Thank you." Emma looked over at the small spring surrounded by large rocks and released soft sigh.

"This isn't your surprise but I am happy you love this view, it's calming." August placed his hand on Emma's lower back and led her toward the spring. "Before you ask, we are not getting wet. I have something a little more date worthy planned." August kept walking with Emma past the spring through the small cluster of trees. When they reached the alcove Emma drew in a noticeable breath.

Twinkling lights, a white linen table cloth and bouquet of pink roses brought a tear to her eye. August had planned and setup a beautiful lunch for just the two of them. There was wine on the table with a tray of fruit and cheeses, there were a few plates with silver domes. Two white chairs were placed on either side of the little table making this feel very intimate.
Was I ready for intimate?
Yes, yes I was ready.

"I wanted to give you something you deserve, something that would put a smile on that beautiful face." August brushed the tear that had escaped from her cheek. "You are worthy of so much more Emma, you deserve the moon and stars and if I could give them to you I would." August pulled out the chair for Emma as he kissed her hand, then sat across from her.

I am always one to do for others, I love doing for others but this, this is nice. The feeling of someone doing something so sweet for me just because, makes me feel special.
"You have no idea how much this means to me. It has been a very trying 24 hours but this distraction is exactly what I needed. How could you possibly know what I needed before I did? You are either psychic or you are heaven sent, care to divulge your secrets?"

"I would love to tell you this is who I am, this is something I do but I can't lie to you. The truth is, I am not this guy. The sweet romantic but with you I find myself needing to be….because it feels right. It feels almost natural for me and having you here, feels very natural. You make me want to be that kind of man, a better man. That is not some sort of line to make you swoon but please feel free to swoon. I think I like the thought, of you swooning over me that is." August smiled at Emma as he uncorked the wine and poured each of them a glass. He had sent this bottle to Letty a few months ago from a vineyard he visited in France. She hadn't opened it and he was not sure he would find something acceptable locally. Not that he was a wine snob but Emma deserved the best. His wine cellar had several bottles from that vineyard but without his assistant right now he had to improvise. He would replace Letty's bottle when he returned to New York.
Return to New York?
Could he return to New York?

"August is there something wrong? You look upset, we can go if you need to."

"There is no other place I want to be Emma, being here with you is everything. I just got lost in thought but you have my full attention. Let's enjoy this meal and take in these picturesque views."

CHAPTER 16

"Mike are you ok? I know this situation with Granny isn't ideal for you but she is too smart and too strong to be fooled by anyone. Letty would never have let him into her life had she thought he would play on her emotions. What really has you so bothered by this?" Gabby was rubbing Mikey's shoulders as she waited for his next patient to arrive.

They had returned to the office after the short visit with Nate and Rachel so they could grab a bite to eat before Mikey had to see more patients. Nate's Doctor decided one more night would be better since Nate wasn't good with his new restrictions. Rachel was released but was staying to make sure Nate listened to the medical staff.

"I honestly don't know why this is bothering me like this. I mean seeing Granny spooning with a complete stranger still haunts me, I don't know if I will ever get that out of my head. I guess I just never thought of her needing anyone like that. I mean, she is Granny not some silver single looking for a hook up, right? Do women even hook up at her age? Wait, don't answer that."

"I couldn't answer that if I tried Mike. I am still a virgin, remember? I think if Granny finds August attractive, enjoys spending time with him, who are we to tell her she can't? They have only just met and the circumstances were pretty traumatic. Maybe it isn't as serious as you think or just maybe it's very serious. Either way don't you trust Granny? The woman did raise three boys on her own and you VanByrne boys are a handful." Gabby smiled and cocked her head at Mikey waiting for his response.

"Maybe you're right. She has always been our rock when we needed her. The voice of reason when we didn't think there was one. I should run upstairs and apologize to her for getting this all wrong." Mikey kissed Gabby on the lips and headed to the kitchen. Granny would be in there creating something for them to eat tonight for dinner. She was always cooking or baking something for them.

When Mikey entered the kitchen he was met with five very feisty kittens. They were everywhere and the mess they were making with the paper towels was insane. Why were they in here? Granny never let them in here when she was cooking. Wait, there were no intoxicating aromas coming from any of the appliances. No sugary smells from any fresh baked pies, no buttery smells from warm biscuits. There wasn't even coffee made today and there was definitely no Granny in here. Looking around Mikey saw the pieces of what appeared to be a note on the floor. From the looks of it, there was a full on tug of war with the paper by these little gremlins. Mikey noticed it was Granny's writing but the only words he could make out made absolutely no sense, late lunch and wait up. Granny wasn't home, she had left a note but only remnants of the note remained. Mikey decided he should just call her phone and see if she was ok, then he would apologize.

Scrolling through his phone he hit call when Granny's name popped up. Waiting patiently as the phone began to ring for her to pick up. Only as the phone rang there was an echo coming from the kitchen causing Mikey to search out the noise. Hanging on the key hook by the door, was Granny's purse and the ringing coming from it meant Granny had not only left her purse but her phone as well!

What the hell has come over her? Granny knows better than to leave the house without her phone. Anything can happen and she had no way to call for help, none! Her car keys were here too which meant she didn't drive anywhere.

August! That guy was causing more harm than good right now and Mikey was not ok.

"Gabby! When is my next patient and how many do I have today?" Mikey was beginning to show his frustration and Gabby was certain he was going to lose it.

"You just had a cancelation, so just one on the schedule for today and he should be here any minute. Did you want to do something today?" Gabby asked softly.

"Yeah, I want to beat an old mans ass! Is there an opening in my day that I can squeeze that in?" Gabby rushed into the kitchen to see if she could calm Mike down.

"Mike, you are not kicking anyone's behind! Granny is a very grown woman and August is a very nice man who isn't a gold digger. Why are you reacting this way? We talked about this, you were ok earlier."

"That was before Don Juan drug her off with no purse, no phone and no way to be reached. What if something happened to Nate? There is no way to reach Granny and this………. this New York playboy has her God knows where, doing God knows what! I don't want to think of the what, help me stop thinking of the what!"

"Don Juan? New York playboy? Mike you have got to stop all this nonsense. You will give yourself a heart attack with all this worry." Gabby was trying to calm a very high strung Mikey, to no avail.

"With no way to reach Granny, jeezus! She would never forgive herself if something happened! See what I mean?" Mikey was beside himself with worry. If this was what having kids was like, he would never be able to procreate!

CHAPTER 17

The stars were beginning to appear faintly in the sky, it was still light out but it was breathtaking. August thought of everything when he planned this little escape. I had forgotten how much this place made you forget the rest of the world and gave you inner peace. I wasn't even sure I needed inner peace but this was everything. We were seated on the big blanket August thought to bring and were looking out over the cliff. Although I had brought a sweater, the heat from August's body was keeping me warm, almost too warm. His strong arm was wrapped tightly around my shoulders and my head resting near his chest. This was the first time in a very long time I felt that being close with someone, I didn't share blood with, was something I needed. August was the first to break our silence.

"You need me to get your sweater? The night air is cooler up here than I had planned for but I really don't want to leave just yet. I am really enjoying the view and the alone time with you." August was looking into my eyes as he spoke and the softness of his gaze reminded me that I was still a woman regardless of my age.

I shook my head in response to his question. I couldn't bring myself to speak words for fear he would hear how he affected me. I felt my body quiver again thinking about our heated kisses and his strong hands. My whole life with Ben had been gentle and sweet and I adored him but August was making me feel things I hadn't felt in a long time or ever.

"Are you ok staying here a little longer? Living in New York for as long as I have, I've missed the stars and the dark canvas of a night sky. The city offers so much but nothing compares to this." August gestured toward the evening sky then looked at Emma. "A beautiful woman, a clear night sky and a big comfy blanket are all a man needs."

"August….." Breathless, I was breathless and I felt my voice quiver. I was glad the sun was setting because I was certain my face was flushed, like a school girl. He was looking into my eyes as he spoke and I felt like he could see my soul.
When his lips crushed against mine I lost all train of thought. The urge to brush away his compliments left and I was returning his kiss with just as much need. I felt my body being laid back on the blanket as August's body covered mine. He was chiseled and strong and his hands were firm and aggressive and when they reached my chest my body bucked in response. His fingers were seeking out the most sensitive parts of me and I couldn't see anything but stars, even with my eyes closed.

"Emma you make me crazy with need and I don't know how to control it. Your lips, your body tell me you need me, when my head should be telling me to slow down. Only….I CAN'T SLOW DOWN! Not with you Emma, I just can't turn this heat between us off." August was resting on his elbows but his body was completely covering me. Before I realized what was happening I felt the night breeze on my bare chest.

"AHEM! You kids need to pack up and head home! This area is closed at dusk and I don't want to bring you in for trespassing this late at night." The voice was familiar but I couldn't look. August was covering me completely with his body as if to protect me from the intruding stranger. I couldn't speak for fear whoever it was would recognize me.
Oh god! I was half naked with a man in a very public place and we have company who may very well recognize me if he sees me! August didn't move from on top of me but looked up at the intruder.

"Aren't you two a little old to play prom night up here? I generally chase off teenagers this late in the evening."

"I wasn't aware we had trespassed, give us a moment to pack up and we will leave." August must have felt my panic, he kept me shielded as he grabbed the corner of the blanket to pull over me. This could be the absolute most embarrassed I have ever been in my life. This interruption was the ice water I needed poured on me to put out the fire I had blazing. If this officer had showed up just 15 minutes later this would have been mortifying, what the hell has gotten into me!

"I will go check the rest of the area but I will be back this way in about 10 minutes. I suggest you take that time to head out. Have a good night you two. Oh….. and Granny? This stays here, no need to mention it to the boys." Gabe (the officer) said with a chuckle.
Kill me now! I go to church with his grandmother and volunteer

at the shelter with his Aunt! This night started out so promising and now I am reminded why this impulsive behavior is a bad idea. A very bad idea!

Gabe left and I immediately started getting myself together, I needed to get home. I needed to figure out how I could fix this. I have never had to worry about what people thought before because I had never given them a reason to question anything about me, until now.

There was a phone ringing in the distance and when it stopped ringing it began ringing again. I realized it wasn't my phone since I had left home without my purse. Another thing I needed to kick myself for. Nate and Rachel couldn't reach me if they needed me because my head was in the clouds and all good sense had left me.

"Letty it's late, what is going on? Are you ok? Are Amy and Rose ok?" August sounded worried as he gathered our things and began loading them into his SUV. I hadn't realized the time until this very moment. We had been here enjoying each other for nearly six hours and I am certain it would have been far longer had Gabe not showed up when he did.
Shit, Gabe!
I am going to have to speak to him about discretion before this gets back to anyone. Good God, I had my 70 year old breasts out in the open, acting like a horny teenager! August Wander turned on his sexy man sorcery and I became a stranger to myself. I have never in my life done anything so bold, so naughty, so…….
…..amazing.

"Emma we need to go, are you ok?" August had finished packing up and was watching me mentally chastise myself. His hand was extended for me to take but I was so wrapped up in my embarrassment I hadn't noticed. He must have finished his phone call with Letty but he looked upset about something.

"Are you ok? Is everything ok with Letty and the girls? Is there anything I can do?" I wasn't sure what had him so upset but if it was anything I did, I needed to fix it. Our time together had gotten out of hand and I hope he wasn't angry with me.

"I am going to need to catch a flight out first thing in the morning. It seems Letty will be bringing both Amy and Rose back with her and my help will be needed. Come with me, we can leave in the morning and stay a night or two then bring the girls back, together." August was almost pleading with me to take off and fly away with him.

I could not do that, could I?

I had Rachel and Nate to take care of. I had Brian and Sarah who might need me, the triplets are so fragile right now in Sarah's tiny frame. Mikey, my sweet little Mikey needed me to help out in his office and those little kittens would miss me terribly. No, I couldn't just run off with August for a few days of......what would it be? Heaven? Sin? Heavenly sin? I am certain a couple days alone with August would be unforgettable but am I ready for unforgettable when he is leaving so soon? His life is in New York and mine is here. Unforgettable sin with August, no matter how brief would most definitely ruin me.

"I am sorry about tonight, I hadn't planned on losing control like that. I have never acted, reacted like that before. It's not who I am, who I have ever been. I can't go with you August, I have too many responsibilities here. I am certain a couple days with you would be amazing but I can't right now. I am sorry." There, that wasn't so hard. Telling him I couldn't be a fling wasn't as hard as I thought it would be, so why did I feel tears burning my cheeks?

"You deserve better than what happened here tonight but I just can't seem to control myself around you. I didn't mean to imply it would be just a couple days Emma. I can't seem to get my fill of you, I am a starving man when I touch you. I don't think I can walk away from you, even if you don't feel the same."

I looked at my hands now placed in my lap as I sat in his passenger seat. The sky was so dark I was sure August couldn't see my face. I didn't know what to say, his words were so honest, so real. I could tell he meant what he was saying but I couldn't let those words change me. I couldn't be the type of woman he was expecting, the kind he was used to, even if I had become one tonight.

"I never said I didn't feel the same way August." It came out like a whisper and I couldn't bring myself to raise my eyes to meet his. He deserved for me to look at him but he would see my tears and I couldn't explain why they were there. I didn't know myself why my tears were falling. Was it the realization that this thing between us couldn't happen? Was it frustration at being caught doing things I knew I shouldn't? Was it the need I still felt but knew I couldn't have filled?

Maybe all the above?

August pulled over and turned to look at me. I couldn't lift my eyes from my lap, not yet. If I saw his face I may just break down and I couldn't let him see that.

"Look at me Em! I know what we were headed for up there was not something we should have been doing. Not there, out in the open and I take responsibility for that. You are just so damn beautiful, I can't seem think straight when I am with you. Last night, when we slept together, I felt like I had held you a hundred times as you slept. Your sleepy face when you woke up was something I want to see more of. I need to see more of. I know we only just met but I feel like I have wasted so much of my life waiting for you that I can't slow down. I have spent so much time documenting perfect that I almost missed finding my perfect. You are my perfect Em. I am not going to be able to walk away."

August was holding my face in his hands using his thumbs to catch my tears. I wanted to tell him I felt the same way. I wanted him to know that his words were what I needed to hear. I wanted to scream when a loud tap on the window scared the hell out of me!

"You two are still in the park and I need you to leave or I will be forced to ticket you."

Damn it Gabe!

This overachiever was working my last nerve! August just looked up at him, nodded his head and pulled onto the road-way. I still hadn't responded to all his confessions, I needed to respond.

"I'm not sure what to say in response to all that. I have so many feelings for you, new unfamiliar feelings. It's been so long August that I am not even sure I remember how this all works. I loved waking up in your arms and tonight…….I loved that too but I can't just leave with you tomorrow. You should go help your family and when you come back, we can pick up where we left off."

Left off? Did I really just say that? Why can't I just beg him to finish what he started? What we started?

"Will you come to Letty's tonight? I can bring you home on my way to the airport. We can talk or sleep or…….anything you're ready for."

My one word answer was out of my mouth before August could finish .

"Yes."

CHAPTER 18

"Brian do you think your ex-wife really thought you would run back to her? I mean, from what you've told me, she was evil." Sarah was enjoying an amazing leg massage while she and Brian sat up in bed. "Not that I am judging, ok I am judging. She was horrible!" Sarah's fingers played with Brian's overgrown hair. When it started to get long the red showed brighter and the ends curled into ringlets. Sarah enjoyed wrapping the curls around her fingers as she rubbed his scalp. Brian seemed to enjoy Sarah's fingers in his hair almost as much as she loved the leg massages.

"We were over long before it was over. Kim was never in the relationship and I guess I accepted it because I was lost……. without you. When I saw you in the ER that night, I just knew I was connected to you. I never felt anything like that for Kim. I cared for her but I guess I never really loved her. Maybe it's my fault she cheated, I wasn't there emotionally but she wasn't you. It's always just been you for me."

"You always say and do all the right things, how's a girl supposed to ever get mad at you?"
"Oh my gosh Brian! The babies, they are kicking. Give me your hand, can you feel it? It feels like a flutter but they are definitely

moving!" Sarah was holding Brian's hands on both sides of her stomach and smiling.

This was the first time the babies were all active at once and it was the most incredible feeling. I knew that getting pregnant was going to be the most amazing experience but having Brian share in this journey was beyond words. Brian had always been her one true love. Even as teenagers she knew Brian was it for her but as time passed she felt alone in that feeling. Brian had never tried to contact her but she hadn't tried very hard either. Now they were married and she would be giving birth to their children. Things between them hadn't taken a very normal route but the result was all that mattered.

"Sarah with these little VanByrne nuggets being this active already we should really think about getting a nursery ready. We haven't done much of anything to prepare for them and time is flying by. I can get someone over here this week to go over ideas but we should decide soon."

"You are such a good daddy and of course you are right. I just haven't given it a lot of thought with working and everything else going on. This house is big enough but I want to keep them together as long as we can. Soon enough the girls will want their space away from their brother and it will just break my heart. We should really start talking about names though, they can hear you call them nuggets." Sarah was laughing as she continued holding Brian's hands on her stomach.

"Let's wait until your next ultrasound and see if we get inspiration. I do not want Brian junior in case you were mulling that around."

"I love name Lincoln but your dads name is really nice. Would you consider Harrison?"

"If I get a say I would like to consider Benjamin in there somewhere. My grandfather was an amazing man and giving that to our son would be pretty special. We can write them all down but we may have to wait until they arrive to get it right. Girls names are just crazy anymore, I think I would like something old school for our girls. Our girls......can you believe we are having three babies?"

"Haha, look at this stomach! There better be three in there!"

The more Sarah thought about it and the size of her stomach, the more that evil bitch Kim's words played over in her head. Her body would be very different after the babies came. Brian loved her and she knew it but would he still want her after the babies came. Newborns can stress a marriage out but three newborns?

"Stop it! That look on your face tells me you are going back to what Kim said. Sarah you are it for me, these babies are it for me. I can't make you unhear her evil words but I can tell you, you are stuck with me FOREVER! Granny doesn't accept returns anyway so you get to keep me." Brian pulled Sarah up onto his chest and kissed her nose.

"You may just be the cutest man I know!"

"Handsome, never call me cute. I am ruggedly handsome and insanely smart, you are welcome." Brian chuckled as he rubbed

Sarah's back and held her to him. They were a perfect fit and nothing was going to change that.

"Ha, still cute!"

The phone ringing caught Brian's attention, it was Mikey. Why was Mikey calling so late?
"Mikey, what's got you up so late? Everything ok?"

"Granny isn't home yet, she has been gone all day! I tried her cell but she didn't take it when she left. I don't like it!"

"She didn't leave a note or text you where she was going? That's odd, even for Granny."

"There was a note but I can't read it. It seems the gremlins were using it as a hacky sac and ate most of it in the process. I made out August and late but nothing else."

"Mikey, I think you got what you need from that. She is with August and she will be out late. Seriously you have got to chill on this. Granny is a big girl, she isn't going to let some guy mess with her head. If she needs us, she knows she has us, she always has us but you have got to relax."

"Fine! I still don't like him and I don't care how much everyone else does."

"Go to bed Mikey, get some sleep and tell Gabby that Sarah wants to do lunch when Rachel gets out of the hospital. They have wedding plans to finish up, remember? You're getting married next month, focus on that."

Before Mikey could respond Brian ended the call shaking his

head. Mikey was going on about Granny's new friend like a crazy man. Sure they only just met but seeing August sit with Granny all day comforting her, this wasn't the actions of a selfish man. He seemed genuine and caring when Granny needed it the most. Mikey had to see that eventually, didn't he?

CHAPTER 19

"Rachel, you up? I can't sleep and I need you to help me get out of this bed for a minute. The nurses are busy so it's now or never. Rachel?"

"Nate I am right next to you and yes I am up. Where do you think you're going? Those same nurses will be back to check your vitals in 15 minutes. What is so important?"

"You, now get me up and in the bathroom, they took my bed controls away the last time I wanted to get up. I think they are plotting to keep me here longer."

"Nate, they are certainly not eager to keep you any longer than they have to. I heard them talking earlier about getting the doctor in first thing to discharge you. You keep trying to get out of bed and are not being a good patient."

"Rachel I need you to help me sit up so I can take you in that bathroom and show my baby momma how much I need her. You help me get out of this bed and I will help you get all tired and cuddly. I love cuddly Rachel."

"Oh my god Nate, you are insane! You are going to get us caught and then banned from this hospital, you know that? We can't keep doing this? They are going to seriously kick me out!"

"Cuddly Rachel is so much happier which of course makes me happier. Just hit the buttons on the bed and I can do the rest, you get what I am saying right?"

"Stop with the sad eyes Nate I will do it, you get what I am saying, right? Rachel winked and began to put the bed down so Nate could make his escape. Watching the light under the door as Nate climbed out of the bed Rachel ran to the bathroom.

"Hurry Nate, we are going to get caught and I am not above faking the whole sleep walking thing again."

"Didn't work the first two times, it isn't going to work now. Come over here and let me feel how my baby is making your body irresistible." Nate grabbed Rachel and pulled her to him caressing her curves and kissing her mouth.

This woman was going to need to get used to me needing her all the time. I knew when I went to that place with her I would never have my fill. I let her inside my head then my heart and that's all it took to consume me. Now that she is carrying my baby, she is going to be my wife sooner than she may want. Our baby is going to grow inside the woman I love.......as my wife.

"Alright you two, time to get back in bed! Nate, we were given strict instructions to pull the power from your bed or strap you down if you got out of bed again. Get out here now, back in bed and I will let it slide.......this time!"

"Shit! Rachel, we are picking this back up tomorrow when we get out of here. We are getting married as soon as we can get a minister to do it. I know you want the whole big beautiful wedding but I won't wait to make you my wife. I need you, the mother of my child, to be Mrs. VanByrne while our baby grows inside you."

"Since you have already given me a proposal that melted my heart, I will let this bathroom proposition slide." Rachel smirked at Nate as she hugged him tightly. "You and I are going to be parents to a wonderful little human. I don't need to have your name Nate but I will be honest with you, I would marry you today if I could."

The knock on the door let Nate know their alone time was over. He grabbed Rachel's hand, opened the door and walked straight over to the bed. He just had to be good until the morning when he would get his release. He could head home with Rachel and heal under Granny's amazing care. He would figure out work later, going back to the firehouse wasn't as appealing as it once was. He had Rachel and now a baby on the way to think about.

"Before you say anything more, I know I should be in bed. I promise to be on my best behavior until I check out of here. I am going crazy in this place! I don't do restrictions well and I am even worse at bed rest. Just tuck me in, give me the tv remote and I promise to stay put." Nate was giving his best puppy dog eyes at the silver haired nurse. Rachel was hiding a smile as she stood behind Nate, holding back a laugh was proving difficult.

"This is the last time I cover for your antics, my next call will be to your Granny. She will be happy to come down and sit with you while you rest. Don't make me get that lovely woman out of bed tonight. STAY. IN. BED! Both of you!"

The nurse, Cora, quickly took Nate's vitals and exited the room. She was a friend of Granny's and was more then willing to do whatever it took to keep Nate in that bed.

"Nate this is serious now, no more alone time until we get home. I can be good if you can." Rachel climbed in Nate's hospital bed and curled into his side. "Let's sleep so we can go home, ok?"

"Fine, sleep. Dream about the wedding we are having….next week. You will be my wife before you have your first doctor appointment." Nate kissed Rachel's hand and slowly drifted off to sleep.

Rachel wanted nothing more than to be Nate's wife but rushing an actual wedding was not going to be easy. It was going to be easier telling her parents about the baby than the rushed wedding. As long as Nate was by her side she knew she could do anything. He was her rock, her protector, her biggest fan and she was all those things for him.

CHAPTER 20

"Brian your phone is ringing, who calls at three in the morning? We don't have to go into the office for four more hours. Wait! Is Nate ok?" Sarah sat up in bed with a panicked look on her face. She had been sound asleep after a long night of baby somersaults when the phone started ringing.

"Let me answer it first, then I will give you all the answers." Brian hadn't been asleep long. He stayed up watching the babies move as Sarah tossed and turned in her sleep. Her sleepy little pleas for calm were as adorable as her face when the babies finally complied.

"Hello Mikey, what has you waking my very pregnant wife way too early?"

"Granny isn't home yet and as you know, she didn't take her phone. I am worried and I have no way to reach her. She must still be with August because I haven't seen her come home yet. What if he is a closet freak and has her tied up somewhere taking underground photos for twisted billionaires?"

"Wait, what? Did you even hear yourself speak? Mikey, Granny is a grown ass woman who may or may not have fallen asleep. You realize that August knows we could end him if he hurt

Granny, right? There is no way anything sketchy is going on, now stop talking to me and go to bed! I have to get my wife back to sleep before the gymnastic team starts up again. Goodnight Mikey."

"He really needs to stop trying to control Granny's life. She is going to get really upset if she finds out he is hunting her down." Sarah moved Brian's hand to her belly where he felt an Olympic team of acrobats warming up. This was going to be a long night for everyone and Brian was pretty sure Mikey was going to get paid back for this.

When Mikey hung up the phone he grabbed his keys and headed out of the house. If Granny was hurt or worse he was not going to be able to live with himself if he didn't help her. Gabby was home so there was no one around to stop him from finding her. The first stop was going to be Letty's house, then the two hotels they had in town.

The streets were dark and there were no other cars on the road but it was after three. Mikey turned onto Letty's street and could see the lights in her house were on. There was a new SUV in the driveway which had to belong to August.
Mikey shut off the lights on his truck and turned into the drive-way. No lights equals no warning and he wasn't giving August any warning.

"Despite the interruption at the overlook today I had an amazing time. I was hoping to continue where we left off earlier but I understand if you would rather not." Emma was seated on the couch with August enjoying a glass of wine. His arm was wrapped around her as she leaned against his chest.

"I was hoping that too but I think I need a little more wine to relax. It's been a long time August and I am afraid I may panic."

"I won't expect anything from you that you aren't comfortable doing. I will gladly wait until you feel you are ready for more. I am content with this right here. A glass of wine, a beautiful woman and an empty house." August reached for the bottle of wine on the coffee table and poured another glass for each of them.

"Sonofabitch! He is going to roofy Granny!"

He has the wine, the empty house and Granny is on the couch looking like his next victim. I need to call Nate!
Shit, I can't call Nate and Brian will kill me if I wake Sarah again.
I can't go in there like a maniac but it's Granny!
If I sit out here and wait for him to make his first move I can stop him before it starts.
Solid plan, sit right here and wait.
I can save Granny before she gets hurt and she will see the care-free philanderer for who he really is.

As long as they don't look outside I am pretty safe right here, out of the way.

Now I just wait.........

"August what time is your flight in the morning? Not that I am rushing you but I would feel terrible keeping you up before such a long flight."

"Letty knows I am coming in the morning, if I miss my flight I can grab the next one. I do not want to rush my time with you, I want to savor it."

Emma felt her heart speed up as August began to gently caress her back. Slowly moving higher with every pass until he reached her neck. His hands made their way to her shoulders where he slowly turned her to him.

This is it Emma, you are going to have this gorgeous man touch you again. Of course you are ready for this, it has been 20 years since you've had a mans touch. Oh god, 20 years. What if I don't remember how this all works, what if I am bad at it! This beautiful man will see me, all of me and I don't even look at all of me, EVER!
What if he doesn't like what he sees, can I handle rejection? How do people do this?

August could see hesitation in Emma's eyes and feel the tension build in her shoulders. He was never one who needed to beg or force a woman to want him and he wasn't going to start now. Emma was too perfect to risk losing her by acting irrational, but he wanted her to be his.

"Emma if this is too soon we can wait. We can just sit here and get to know each other. I promise you I am ok with whatever we do or don't do." August began gently kissing Emma's neck and running his fingers down her collarbone. If she was fine with light petting, he was going to pet.

"I am afraid I may not know enough, anything really. It's been so long and I am afraid to disappoint you but trust me, my body wants this. My mind isn't on board yet but I am praying it catches up soon, very soon."

"Please don't think for a minute you could ever disappoint me. You have me wrapped up completely and nothing, I mean nothing we share will be less than perfection."
August gently laid Emma back on the couch as he positioned himself over her small frame. Trailing kisses down her throat taking small bites as he moved down to her chest. Taking in her scent as he unbuttoned her blouse, she smelled of fresh lilacs and tasted like the sweetest vanilla. He never thought a smell could intoxicate him but Emma was intoxicating. Having her even in the smallest of ways was going to ruin him for other women.

"I am trying to go slow, trying to be good, you deserve good but you are driving me crazy. I need you Emma, I need you like a desert needs rain."

Well those were all the right words because my mind was now cheering him on. I was really going to do this.
I moved August's left hand to my waist and gently moved it south as his right hand grabbed my breast. His kisses became hungry as his tongue found mine. I was moving frantically to get him to touch everything all at once. The proof of how my body was affecting him pressed firmly on my core. I needed to be closer to him, I needed his heat, his skin, I needed August.

Just when I thought my body couldn't take anymore I felt

August pull away. He stood before me and pulled me up to him. The cool air on my skin alerted me that I was once again bare from the waste up, I hadn't even felt that happen. I wanted to cover my nakedness but when I saw the look in August's eyes as he studied my body, I felt unashamed. I had never felt more desired and I wanted to be desired.

With his hand on my lower back he led me to his room. I had been in this house hundreds of times but in this moment everything seemed foreign. The click of the door closing was like the starting pistol of a race. I felt his hands pull off my remaining clothing as lips traced my curves. I found myself pulling at his shirt so I could feel his skin on mine. Before I could beg, we were naked and fumbling our way to the bed. The urgency took over as we began exploring each other. I needed more, more of his mouth on me, more of his hands all over me. I was lost in this moment and didn't recognize who I had become. With one thrust I felt my soul leave my body and be replaced with a million tiny firecrackers. I couldn't control what was happening and I couldn't stop my bodies reaction. I was completely claimed by this handsome man and I had no idea how I would recover from it.

Could I recover from it?

August was kissing the bottoms of my feet when my eyes opened for the first time. The light was just beginning to peak in the window solidifying the fact that we had spent the night together. Judging by the tenderness of every one of my muscles, we hadn't slept through much of it.

"I missed my first flight but my next one is in two hours. I would cook for you but I can't even boil water. If you can climb out of this bed I will take you to breakfast. If you stay there much longer I will miss the next three flights." August was smiling as he climbed back onto the bed. He must have gotten up really early if he slept at all. He was showered, dressed and smelled amazing.

"Do I have time to shower first? I can wait until I get home if you are in a hurry."

"You shower but I need to leave the house while you do or we aren't going anywhere today. I have a few things I grabbed from Letty's closet you can wear already on the chair. Now hurry off or you won't be getting fed and I won't be flying anywhere." Emma got up quickly and ran to the bathroom as August headed outside. He needed to throw an overnight bag in the car for his flight anyway.

As August opened the front door he noticed a second vehicle in the driveway. Once he got closer he found Mikey asleep at the wheel. With a light tap on the glass Mikey jumped awake and looked around in a panic.

"If you are looking for Emma she is in the shower. If she doesn't know you're here you may want to leave now. You and I can talk about this when I return in a couple days. I do not want Emma upset, especially if I am not here to help her." August was speaking softly but Mikey could tell he was not happy.

"Sorry, I was worried about her. She didn't have her phone and

I couldn't reach her. I must have fallen asleep waiting for her. Look, don't say anything to her about me being here. I have to get home for work, we can talk when you come back." Mikey was hoping August didn't come back. Maybe he would just go back to New York and leave Granny alone.

She had he and his brothers, she didn't need August. He would only break her heart, wouldn't he?

CHAPTER 21

Mikey: *Guys we need a family meeting, like right now!*

Brian: *Do you copy paste this shit? Why do we need a meeting now?*

Mikey: *I messed up and I think I pissed off that August guy.*

Gabby: *Mike, what did you do? I told you to just get some sleep, that Granny was fine.*

Nate: *What the hell guys? I am waiting on the Doctor to release me. Can you wait to go over your middle school drama?*

Brian: *Ok, how did you piss him off and are you sure you did or just think you did?*

Mikey: *I know I did! I couldn't find Granny, she didn't have her phone so I drove to Letty's. She was there with HIM! I was waiting for her to come out but she didn't. I thought he roofied her so I was going to save her but I fell asleep waiting for the lights to go out.*

Nate: Oh shit! Why would you think he roofied her? What did you see?

Mikey: I saw wine and a couch and an empty house!

Brian: Mikey, that's a date not a frat party. What were you thinking? Does Granny know? Because if she does, you are in serious trouble.

Nate: I am getting an IV taken out and laughing my ass off at this. Mikey you need to chill. Granny has us if she needs us…. IF. SHE. NEEDS. US.

Mikey: *August woke me and told me to leave. He said we would talk when he gets back in a couple days. What should I do?*

Sarah: *One- figure out how to delete this group text from Granny's phone! Wrong chat group….again. Two- start working on your apology to both of them. Three- take Nate's advice (just this once, sorry Nate) and chill the hell out! Sorry, no sleep because the soccer team in my uterus is training for the olympics! Brian I need a foot rub!*

Mikey: *Son of a bitch, quick- what's Granny's phone password?*

Rachel: *My 5 gremlins:) good luck Mikey!*

"Nate you will need to have your stitches removed in 7 to 10 days. You are healing nicely and with such a clean cut there should be minimal scarring." Dr. Manuel was going over Nate's discharge orders and follow up care with both Rachel and Nate. "You will need to see Dr. Andi for your fracture and probably schedule some rehab but you are one lucky man. I hope this is a wake up call and you are a little more cautious with your future endeavors. I can send this all over to Brian if you'd like, I am assuming he will take over as your primary?"

"I got it doc, trust me I am not coming back. I have all the information and will follow everything. I am good with Brian getting my file too. Can we get out of here now? I am starving and could use a good meal." Nate shot Rachel a crooked grin and a smoldering wink as Dr. Manuel chuckled. She knew everything about Nate's stay because the nurses were thorough in documenting everything.

"Fine, let me get you a chair and before you say anything else……..you ARE taking a ride down to the doors. Rachel, Brian has your car in the employee lot next to the exit. You both need to take it easy and don't do anything to worry that sweet grandmother of yours."

Nate climbed into the wheelchair as the orderly took him out ahead of Rachel. Nate hated not being able to leave on his own two feet but he was happy to be leaving. He couldn't wait to get home and not have to worry about the constant interruptions from the nurses. He and Rachel had planning to do and Nate was going to start making calls. This wedding was going to happen and it didn't matter what anyone else thought.

The ride home was quiet as Rachel replayed everything in her head. She was carrying Nate's baby. They were getting married soon and she almost lost him. The events of the last few days were catching up to Rachel as a soft flow of tears escaped. If you would have said a year ago that she was going to be getting married and having the baby of this beautiful caring man, she would have thought you were crazy. Now it all just seemed dreamlike. No man had ever made her feel this loved, this complete or needed. Now she was going to be a wife and mother because of this man.

Before Rachel even had the chance to put the car in park, Nate was out of the car and at her door. He placed his thumbs on her cheeks to brush away the trails of moisture and kissed her lips. "I never want to be the reason your cheeks need drying but I will always be there to dry them."

"Damn it Nate, now I am going to cry again. I love you so much that everything just caught up with me. I think my hormones are messing with my tear ducts so get used to this new look I have going on." Nate helped Rachel out of the car and into the very quiet house. They were met by five very active kittens who were attacking everything that moved. It was clear Granny was not home yet so Rachel began gathering the little crew and placing them in the den. It was pretty apparent why Guido slept all the time when the babies started pulling his ears and biting his tail. Poor guy took it like a champ while Lou just watched from the window, out of reach.

"Granny isn't home yet, can I get you anything to eat? You must be starving by now." Rachel asked as she closed the den doors. "We could order in and eat in bed, it's almost lunch time anyway."

"Oh I am a starving man but not for food. Let's go upstairs and spend some non rushed quality time together. We can eat later, much later."

"We need to discuss this wedding and call my parents Nate. I can't wait to cuddle up in that big ole bed but we have to figure out what we are doing. I am good with city hall, if I get a vote." Rachel winked as she grabbed their bag and headed for the stairs.

Before her foot hit the first stair Nate had the bag in his hand and was pulling Rachel up behind him. If they were going to plan a wedding and it would be a wedding, it was going to be memorable.

"I will call reverend Landis while you call your parents. We are getting married next Saturday and I don't care who can't make it. We will have it here, no booking conflicts and Granny would love it. You ready to become Mrs. VanByrne?" Rachel smiled at Nate and nodded her head, she was very ready to make this happen. Calling her parents and telling them was another story.

CHAPTER 22

"You didn't need to take the time to feed me August, I can cook remember. It is a nice change though and I did work up quite an appetite." Emma smiled shyly as she took a drink of her coffee. They had stopped at a small diner on their way to the airport to grab breakfast. Strangely enough there were no forced conversations or awkward feelings between them. After everything they had done earlier, it seemed very natural between them.

"I wasn't ready to let you go just yet. I want every available moment with you Emma. I wish I didn't have to leave but Letty needs me to help bring Amy back with her. It seems that Amy's choice in a father for her new baby isn't worthy of the breath he draws. Let's not talk about them though, I really want to discuss us."

"Us or this morning?" Emma spoke softly as she watched for August's reaction.

"Emma, I want to talk about us. If we talk about this morning, I am not getting on a plane. I want, no I need, you to know that what we shared was nothing like I have ever experienced before. I am not just talking about the physical part, which was amazing, I am talking about the emotional connection we shared. Since I met you I have had this need to be near you and I don't think that's ever going to go away. It is killing me to leave you even for a couple days. I know you have obligations here but I really want you to come with me. We can stay a couple extra days and enjoy each other, no distractions. Maybe go to New York and see a show or just take in the sites. I want to share everything I am with you, I want you to know everything about me. I want to know everything about you as well, your passions, all the things you don't like. Emma, I need more of you and I am ready to do whatever it takes to get it."

"August I can't go with you. Nate and Rachel are getting out of the hospital today and I need to make sure they are ok. Those boys have been my life since the day they were born. Then when they lost their parents we were all they had. When Ben died I was the only person they had left and they were all that was left of my only child. I do feel the same way about you but right now I am needed here. You need to take some time to get Letty and Amy home. We can see each other when you come back. Frankly I could use the time to get myself together. I feel like I am in a dream state and just need to get my feet back down to earth."

August smiled in acknowledgement at what Emma was saying but deep down he was wounded. The time they spent together last night and this morning sparked emotions he had never felt before. Although he was hesitant at first to take things as far as they did, it was the soft moans and pleading looks Emma gave him that turned him into a desperate man. One he didn't recognize but one he would not regret becoming. Emma was everything he had ever hoped to find in a woman. She was sweet, funny, loving and beautiful, God was she beautiful. The thing was, she didn't even realize how captivating she was and if she did know, she didn't show it. Of all the beautiful, perfect women he had photographed, spent time with, he never once felt the way Emma had him feeling. Leaving here, leaving her was going to gut him when he had to return to New York. Why the hell did he only take two weeks? What would happen if he extended his stay? Could he take more time away from work? Emma was definitely worth whatever price there was to pay. He had to make some calls when he got to Georgia, this was going to work out, it had to.

"August we really should get going, you still need to check in for your flight. You can turn in your rental and I can call Mikey for a ride. You shouldn't pay rental on a vehicle you are not using, I don't need it."

"I have seen your car Emma, I would feel much better about you driving the rental. I have it paid for and will need it when I return anyway. It is so hard leaving you after so little time together." August waived over the waitress to get the bill. When she handed him the check he handed it back with a 100 dollar bill.

"The change is yours if you can do me one favor. Take a couple photos of us with my phone. I need to see this beautiful face every day I am gone, to remember how lucky I am." August handed his phone to the waitress who placed her hand to her heart and nodded her head.

"You two are the most adorable couple I have ever waited on. I have been here for a lot of years and no one has ever looked at a woman the way you look at her. I would be happy to document this for you. Makes me believe in love just seeing you two together."

Love, oh my goodness!
Is what I feel for August love?
How do I even know what that feels like anymore? I can't be in love it's been what, a couple days? He has a life in New York and I have my life here. I have great grand babies coming and two weddings to plan. Do I even have time for love? Do we have time for love?

"Smile!"
August's lips were on mine so fast I couldn't remember what I was thinking about. We were having our pictures taken by a lovely woman one second then I was feeling his molars with my tongue the next. Once his teeth bit gently on my lip I was lost in August. If we didn't get out of here soon this waitress and these patrons were going to have a very different opinion of us. An opinion that was far from G rated!

August pulled away first and placed his hand on my lower back to lead me out of the diner. He had gotten his phone back but I can't remember seeing that happen. This is occurring a lot when he is around. I need to ask Brian if there is a form of amnesia that only comes on when you are ummm..........happy.

"Emma I feel like a man in his 20's when I am with you. I find it very hard to keep my hands off of you and when we kiss? I just can't control myself, this trip is going to kill me. Type your number into my phone and I will send you these photos, just in case you might miss me too." Emma took the phone and sent a text to her phone. It was still at home but she would get them when she got back to her house. She was really going to miss August but these pictures would help.

"I just sent myself a text so you have my number and I have yours. Before you go I just want you to know that I have really loved spending time with you. I already can't wait until you come back." I really hope that didn't come out as desperate as it sounded.

Was I desperate for this, for August?

I can absolutely confirm.......I am desperate for more August.

CHAPTER 23

"I need to see Brian, it's important. Think you could do your job and let him know I am here?"

Sarah looked up from the desk she was seated at to see Kim had once again showed up at Brian's office. She was looking bored and oozing with condescension but Sarah wasn't going to cause a scene for the two patients waiting, so she walked back to Brian's office to warn him.

"Brian, your ex-wife is here again and she is sharpening her fangs in the waiting area. She insists on seeing you but you do have two patients waiting."

"She is relentless! Can you bring her back here, this should be quick since I have nothing to say to her. I don't want you to to leave either, I want you here with me in case I need an alibi." Brian winked at Sarah as she turned to leave his office.

Taking a deep breath Sarah opened the hall door and asked Kim to follow her back to Brian's office.

"You can go back to your desk now, I know the way to his office. You aren't needed for anything and your feet are huge, you should probably get off them."

Jeezus this woman was a bitch, like an evil, nasty bitch. Brian won't need the alibi, I will! This woman has breathed the same air as me a total of two times now and I want to choke it right out of her! This isn't pregnancy hormones playing with my emotions, this is a bitch in stilettos spiking my last nerve!

"Kim, why are you here? We have nothing to discuss and you are not welcome here. Your only in my office to save my patients from your theatrics." Brian was attempting to keep his cool but the look he was getting in return was challenging him.

"She isn't involved in this" Kim waived her finger from Brian to herself while glaring at Sarah "she can leave while we talk."

Oh hell no, this was not going down like this! This bitch was not dismissing me, Brian's wife, mother of his children like some old take out! It's a good thing I am wearing slippers because the heals would be flying if she looked at me again.
"Kim do not EVER speak to or about the woman I love with such disrespect again. I will not tolerate it or you, so please see yourself to the door marked EXIT. Also, on your way out try forgetting your way here. If you come here again I will have you banned from the building, then arrested for trespass. Am I clear or should I put it in writing for you?"

"You can't Brian, I am working in this building. That's why I came here, to tell you I am working with Dr. Kabre in his office. You will be seeing a lot of me, since your wife is a patient there."

Sarah felt her stomach roll and the air leave her lungs. How the hell does this happen? What kind of sick, twisted woman gets a job to……. do what exactly? What was she trying to do by working in her OB's office? This can't be real, it can't be happening!

"Say what? You got a job in this building? Working for a doctor who is taking care of my wife and children, for what purpose? Are you insane?"

"Brian it's a job, I needed a job and I saw a sign when I was here before so I applied. I was informed today that I got the job. I do not need your permission to work here but as you can see, banning me from the building isn't possible. I will be here every day so we will run into each other. I wanted to tell you myself before you bumped into me." Kim was now enjoying herself and the obvious stress she was putting on Sarah.

Fuuuuuuuuck me! The bitch was working for my doctor, my OB! What in the hell am I going to do now? There is no way I am going into that office with that bitch reading my file!
Oh shit no!

"Looks like I need to speak with Dr. Kabre then. I won't have you interfering in my wife's care or snooping into her personal file. Are there no limits to the bullshit you stoop to? This is definitely a low Kim, even for you."

"Brian don't! I need a job and this one will help me get back on my feet. I can't lose it before I even start. I know you moved on, I do and you're finally getting the children you always wanted.... with her."

"Stop! I mean it Kim! I will call Dr. Kabre right now! Sarah is my wife and I love her with everything that I have, you need to respect that."

"Fine! Don't ruin this job for me Brian, I need it. Your wife's file doesn't interest me and I won't jeopardize my job. Just don't do anything, please."

I just realized I have been stunned into silence for this whole conversation. What was playing out in front of me was every nightmare I had ever had, wrapped up and thrown like a brick through a church window. It was horrifying to think that the beautiful moments Brian and I were going to share with these babies was going to be tainted by Kim's pure evil. I need to say something, I had to put a stop to this crazy. Why was this all happening to us? What in the hell did he even see in this spawn of Satan?

"Thank you Brian, I will see myself out. I guess I will see you around."

Shit! What just happened and how did I miss it? I was so busy with the bullshit in my head I missed what they discussed! Kim looked unfazed as she left, why was she unfazed? I am very fazed by this situation and Brian had better of taken care of it! Please God let Brian have taken care of it!

"Sarah, honey are you ok? Do you need to sit down for a minute?" Brian had led Sarah back to his desk and had her sit on the corner of it.

"Brian I may have some pregnancy hormones playing with my head but what just happened? I seem to remember your ex-wife saying she is working for my OB? Brian please tell me I didn't hear that, tell me you fixed the issue because I am thinking lunch is going to make an appearance in a less than appealing form. Tell me she is not working here, tell me my OB who specializes in multiple births is not employing that evil bitch! I really need you to tell me Brian, tell me I imagined it all."

"Sarah."

"Oh no! Don't you dare tell me she is working there, in that office! Don't you dare tell me I have to see that bitch each time we get to see these babies because I will not have her turn this beautiful moment into ......into, oh my God!"

"Sarah she is working in his office, that doesn't mean she will be part of this, part of our journey into parenthood. We are having three beautiful babies under the care of an exceptional doctor. I will see what can be done to limit or avoid her interactions with us but this doctor really is important to us."

Did I really just hear Brian correctly? Is he really trying to pacify me on this? There is no way in hell I am going to be ok with this, ever! I will find another doctor before I let this bitch taint my pregnancy. She is insane, that is the only explanation, she is certifiable! I should speak, say something to Brian but I can't get my mouth to work. I feel like this is happening to someone else and I am a silent observer. I did the only thing I could do.......I ran to the bathroom to cry, throw up and repeat those steps all over again in that very order.

"Sarah, honey are you ok? Can I come in?" Brian was poking his head in the door of the small bathroom.

Why didn't I lock the door? Because I was too upset, that's why!

I cannot have this conversation here at the office. There are too many things I want to say but this is not the place.

"I will be but I need to go home for the day. We can talk when you get home but I need to go." I couldn't even raise my head to look at him. I felt him staring at me waiting for more but I wasn't ready for that. I heard the door click shut as he left so I waited a little bit before I stood up. I saw my face in the mirror and realized I needed to clean up before I left. I would shoot Brian a text after I grabbed an Uber. One of the bad things about riding to work together when you have a break down in the office, grabbing a ride home from a complete stranger.

CHAPTER 24

"Good news wife to be, I have a minister who is available and as soon as Granny gets home I will have the venue. How is it going with your parents? Are they able to make the trip?" Nate was laying in bed as Rachel walked into the bedroom holding her cell phone.

"They literally just told me they won't be able to make it. My mom has to have surgery in two days and it is something that can't be rescheduled. She won't be able to make the trip, even if they flew in. I feel bad because I don't want to wait but I really want them here." Rachel was holding back tears as she sat next to Nate on the bed. She had always been close with her family, even though she had been away from them so much. Rachel had not really been back home since she started college, she started working right after graduation. Not having them here for her big day was never something she had entertained. They seemed very excited about becoming grandparents but them not being able to come to the wedding was disheartening.

"Sweetheart I know having your parents at our wedding is important to you but I really want to be selfish here. I want to be your husband and I honestly don't need anybody to witness it. If it's just you, me and the minister I would be the happiest man on earth. I understand if you want to wait but I really want you as Mrs. Nate VanByrne and I am praying like hell you agree." Nate sat up, pulled Rachel into his arms and kissed the top of her head. "I love you so much and I want the world to know that we belong to each other. The caveman in me wants to claim you today but I am trying to be good here."

"I want all that too Nate, it sucks that my parents won't be here but I am going to marry you as planned. Maybe,when you are feeling better, we can make a trip to Illinois. We can spend some time with my family so they can fall in love with you too." Rachel curled into Nate as he held her to him. He would do anything she asked of him, even if he wasn't feeling up to it.

"We will get married, then we can make plans to go see your family. We can stay a few days and you can feed me that amazing pizza you told me so much about. I would even consent to a shopping trip on the magnificent mile, if it meant seeing you happy."

"I am happy Nate, I have you and this little VanByrne right here." Rachel was rubbing her stomach and smiling at Nate. "I don't need anything else to make me happy."

There was a light tap on the door and Granny's voice followed "Can I come in you two"?

Granny was back home now and would be smothering these two with food and attention.

"Yes, please come in Granny." Nate wanted to tell her about the wedding as soon as possible. He was making sure they had enough time to get everything right.

"You both look wonderful but I bet you're hungry for something home cooked. Let me head to the kitchen and start on lunch for you."

"Granny we are hungry but I need to tell you something first. Rachel and I want to get married next week, right here. Do you think we could make that happen? I have the minister we just need everything else." Nate smirked knowing Granny would see to it that the wedding did happen and was flawless.

"Well I guess I better get my phone and start making calls. Rachel when are your parents arriving? I can get a room ready for them to stay here if they would like."

"Ummm, they can't make it. They wanted to but mom is having surgery in two days and won't be able to make the trip. Nate and I will take time after the wedding to go see them. It's fine, really, I am not waiting to marry your grandson." Rachel gave Granny a half smile and let out a small sigh.

"Well alright then, let's get these plans rolling. Do you have your dress already? If not I can help with that too."

"Oh no! I didn't even think about a dress. I will never be able to order one in time and having one made will be impossible." Rachel was looking panicked just talking about the dress. Granny was going to need to do a lot of this planning, stress was not good for the baby.

"You come with me and we will see what we can do about that. I have lots of treasures we can work with and if that doesn't work, I think I can make a call." Granny didn't want to ask August for help but if it meant Rachel would have a dress on her big day, she was ready to start dialing. She still had her own wedding dress sealed and put away in addition to Nate's mothers dress. Since Rachel isn't really showing yet the dresses should fit her just fine, if she wanted to wear one of them.

Granny made it to her room and opened the large closet where she had several boxes stacked. She would just pull them out and let Rachel look them over.

"I have my wedding dress in this box and Nate's mothers dress in that box, so let's see what we have. You do not need to pick either of them, this is your day and we will get you the dress you were meant to wear."

Rachel opened the first box, it contained a satin dress with beautiful detail on the train. There were pearls sewn into the neckline that gave it an elegant feel. Granny's dress was gorgeous but it was very white. Rachel had hoped for ivory, if she had a choice.

She grabbed the 2nd box and was shocked to see a mermaid style strapless gown in ivory. The dress was completely made out of intricate lace with an open back. Surely this wasn't an older dress, it was stunning.

"This dress is everything I pictured for my wedding day. This can't be an older dress, it looks like it could be on the rack today."

"It was timeless when I helped my daughter pick it out. Seeing it brings back such beautiful memories but I would love some new ones too. Let's see how it fits, I can do the alterations if we need to." Granny laid the dress on her bed and unzipped the back. The last time she touched this dress was to help her daughter marry the man of her dreams. The look on Harrison's face as Evie made her way down the aisle was one of pure love. Evie loved this dress and one day wanted to pass it down to her daughter. Since she was blessed with all boys I think she would love to have Rachel wear it as she started her life with Nate.

Granny slipped the dress over Rachel's head as she shimmied into the bodice. The lace poured down Rachel's body before it came to rest on her hips. Granny stepped behind Rachel to zip the dress up while Rachel held the top in place. As Granny pulled the tiny white zipper head she was flooded with memories. Memories of Ben walking Evie down the aisle. The father daughter dance and love in eyes as he gave her hand to Harrison.

"It's beautiful, like it was made for you. Look in the mirror, you are a vision my dear girl. If you don't feel the same way it won't offend me but sweetheart you look gorgeous."
Rachel's eyes met the mirror and Granny's reflection as she took in the dress she was wearing. A tear escaped her eye as the realization set in, she was going to marry Nate, in his mother's wedding dress. The dress his mother wore when she started her life with his father.

"Rachel there is something else I need to show you on the dress but I want to be certain you want it before I do. Should I prepare to take you shopping for one or will you become Nate's wife in his mother's gown?"

"Granny it is beautiful and I want this to be the dress Nate sees me in when we exchange our vows." Rachel's eyes filled with more tears as she ran her hands over the delicate lace.

"I am so happy Rachel, this dress isn't just Evie's dress though." Granny lifted the all lace train up and brought it around to the front. "This train was added after Evie picked this dress out. The lace panel that creates this beautiful train was my mothers veil. Evie wanted part of her grandmother with her when she married Harrison. You have to really look close to see the difference in the lace but it was important to her. We had the dressmaker in town work her magic and there you have it." Granny was running her fingers over the lace as she admired the dress.

"I don't even know what to say. I mean this dress is a family heirloom and you are letting me wear it on the most special day of my life. I just don't have words to describe how happy this makes me. I really wish my mother were here but I am really glad I have you. There is one little thing I would like to ask and you can say no.......I would love to add a tiny part of your dress to this one. If I had a little bit of each of you with me, it would make our day that much more special."

Granny smiled and nodded afraid to speak, not because she was unsure but because if she spoke she was certain she would cry. Rachel had not only taken Nate's heart but a big part of Granny's in the few short months they had known her.

CHAPTER 25

"Mike we need to talk about who will replace my free labor in this office. You have enough patients coming in daily that you need a full time assistant. I will be going back to teaching soon and I need to get my classroom ready. I think it will be too much for Granny to take on full time."

"Shit, Granny! I hate that I am being such an ass about this guy she is obviously seeing. Problem is……I think he might even be a decent guy and I just keep…..ugh"
Mikey was holding his head in his hands as he sat at his desk. When this guy got back into town he knew he had to face him and straighten everything out, for Granny's sake.

"Mike, he has a name and he seems like a nice guy. You are going to have to fix this situation before you hurt Granny. She loves you guys and she would do anything for each one of you. Don't you think it's time you guys start doing the same?"

"Umm, wow Gabby. Don't you think that is what this is? Doing everything we can to protect her, protect her heart, keep her safe."

"I think you got that wrong Mike, try being team Granny for a change and maybe cheer her on. She has been alone a lot of years, you guys aside, don't you think she deserves more? Don't you think she is ready for more?"

What is Gabby even talking about? Granny doesn't need more, she has all of us! Ok, maybe she needs more friends since we are all busy with life but does it need to be a guy? That guy? I mean he doesn't live here, he is only here for what, a couple weeks? Enough time to break her heart then run back to New York, back to his models. Back to his big penthouse and elite social circles.

Wait, he is only here for a couple weeks! He has already been here like two, three days, that leaves just over one week left. Just eleven more days of......August!

"Look sweetheart, as much as I don't want to admit you're right, just maybe you are right. Maybe I have been looking at this all wrong. Granny could use a friend to have dinner with while we are all out. He isn't planning on being here all that long and Granny could use a friend at least until Letty returns. How much harm can he really do in just eleven more days?"

"See, doesn't that feel better? Getting all that out and rationalizing it like an adult. We still need to talk about my replacement. I have two weeks before I need to start getting my classroom ready, so maybe we should place an ad in the paper. I can help with the interviews and even the training before school starts again."

"I will talk to Granny first and then decide if we need an ad. I don't want her to see the ad and not want to be replaced. I have already reacted badly on just about everything concerning

Granny so maybe it's time I think this through first."

Gabby nodded her head in acknowledgement while flashing a small smile. Mike was coming around and it was about time.

Footsteps coming down the stairs alerted Mikey and Gabby they had company coming to the kitchen.

"Hello you two, are you hungry? I need to do some serious baking today. Letty will be coming home and she is bringing Amy and that new grand baby with her. It sounds like they will be staying so I thought I would help her out a little bit. A few casseroles and some cobblers should get them started."

"Hey Granny, you said Amy is coming back? For good? You think she would need a job? I could use a little help since Gabby is going back to teaching and I feel terrible about locking you behind a desk all day." Mikey was hoping August hadn't told Granny about this morning but if he kept her talking, he would definitely know.

"Oh lord Mikey, you need to hire someone. I can't be trapped like an animal in a cage, I have stuff to do. I have babies to get ready for, a couple weddings to help with. With Nate and Rachel getting married next week, I have a million things to do."

"I may have not heard you correctly but did you say Nate and Rachel are getting married next week? Like seven days from now?" Mikey was caught off guard by this news flash.

"Well actually, the wedding is next Saturday and I have a ton of things to do before then. It will be here in the garden so planning won't be that difficult. We did just have Brian's here not that long ago. To answer your initial question, I guess Amy will be looking for a job but she did just have a baby so she won't be ready right away." Granny smiled brightly at them as she began gathering supplies. She was going to spend the next couple days in the kitchen, keeping her mind and hands busy not thinking about August being gone.

August, the pictures! I need to grab my phone and look at the pictures from this morning. I will need to save those, they hold really nice memories for me no matter how this all ends. It will end and I will be sad to see him go but the time he has given me was worth whatever pain I will have to eventually endure.

Granny reached into her purse but could not find her phone. That's strange I always keep it in my purse.
"Mikey can you call my phone? I must have misplaced it but I have no idea where. If you call it I should be able to hear it ring."

Shit! Granny's phone is in my office because I had to delete my group text. If I call it she will know I was snooping.

"You sure you didn't leave it in the den? Why don't you head that way and I will call it for you."

Granny headed to the den as Mikey ran back to his office. All he had to do was grab the phone and put it in the kitchen before he called it. Easy, right?

Mikey made it back to the kitchen and dialed Granny's phone as he looked around for a spot. Just as he was heading into the pantry Granny came back. He was standing in the doorway holding both phones as Granny's phone started to ring.

"Oh Granny, I was just going to yell for you. I ummmm, found your phone in the pantry. I heard the vibration before it rang. You may want to be more careful where you leave it, these kittens are like mountain goats and I would hate for them to break it." Mikey was breaking out in a cold sweat, praying she bought his story.

"Your ears must bionic, I couldn't hear a thing. Thank you dear and I could have sworn it was in my purse. Oh well, I need to check on those little darlings then start my baking. You kids ok for today? Do you need anything?"

"We're good until lunch, thanks Granny. Gabby we have patients coming, we better head into the office."

"I will have lunch ready soon you two, oh and Mikey? You are a terrible liar but I have things to do and a wedding to plan so I will let it slide, this time." Granny winked at Mikey and started scrolling through her phone to check her messages. August's photos were on her phone. They brought a smile to her face as she placed her fingers on her lips, remembering the way his lips made hers feel.
A new message appeared as she was saving the photos to her phone.

August: *Just wanted to tell you that I miss you already. I have a couple hours in the air but be ready when I land because I want to hear your voice before we go to bed tonight.*

Granny: *I will keep my phone with me until you return. I love the photos you insisted on this morning, I am saving them in case I for-*

get what you look like.

Granny smiled as she typed the last sentence knowing August wouldn't see it until after he landed. He would be calling her anyway, it would be a definite conversation starter.

August: *Not funny, plane hasn't taken off yet. We will talk about that when I call you tonight. You will have to figure out how to help repair my wounded heart. The stewardess is hovering over me now so I have to turn my phone off. I will miss you…..*

CHAPTER 26

Thankfully my last patient was just a simple physical so charting it up was quick. I needed to get home to Sarah, she wouldn't answer the phone all day. I know she was upset because of Kim but we can get through this. I just need to talk to her and smooth this out. If I need to talk with Dr. Kabre about this I will, my wife and children will always come first. I can't let Kim cause Sarah any stress and I would really rather not have to see Kim daily.

The chime from the elevator and the whoosh of the doors were welcomed as I made my quick entrance. I was hitting the ground floor button harder than necessary when I heard I had company. I turned to acknowledge my travel companion and possibly explain myself when I saw Dr. Kabre smile and nod.

"Where is that wife of yours? Not taking the stairs I hope, she needs to continue to take it easy."

"She actually left early today which is why I am in such a hurry to get home. She wasn't feeling very well after we met your new employee today."

"New employee? I don't recall having a new employee in the office today. We had a few interviews but I don't expect any new faces for a few weeks. It's been pretty busy in the office so I thought I would bring on another nurse and maybe a technician. I just hate overworking my team when we can just add staff."

"Kim isn't either of those, are you sure you aren't looking to add another position?"

"Kim? Kim Kelley? She was definitely in my office today trying to get a file room position but I don't need any staff in there. She was very insistent on her qualifications but I am in no way bringing her on. My staff is like family and I got the feeling she wasn't a family kind of employee. Do you know her?"

"You could say that, she was my wife for a brief time. Best thing I ever did was to move on from that train wreck. It's very strange that she made a point to tell me she was going to be working for you. It really makes no sense but it's also odd that she gave you her maiden name. I think it's safe to say you and I both dodged that bullet."

The doors to the elevator opened at the ground floor as Brian made his way to the car. Still not able to shake the events of today or the information he just learned in the elevator. What in the hell is Kim trying to do here? Was this just some sick plan to upset us? I need to get home and tell Sarah everything, maybe she can make sense of this crazy shit.

The drive home was short but long enough to have Brian rushing into the house in a panic because of the irrational thoughts running through his head.

"Sarah honey, you home? I have tried to call you all day but you aren't answering my calls."

Realizing Sarah was not downstairs Brian took the stairs two at a time and swung the bedroom door open. The loud clatter from the door hitting the wall startled a very sleepy Sarah curled up in their bed.

"What the hell! Brian you scared the shit out of me! Why are you making so much noise? Annnnd the summersaults are starting again." Sarah groaned and grabbed her stomach. Brian rushed to her side and held her hands looking at her eyes for any pain. "Sarah I am so sorry about today, I just didn't know what to do. You and these babies will always come first, you are my world. That whole run in caught me off guard, I had patients but I wanted to be here holding you. I tried to call all day but you weren't taking calls, I am so sorry sweetheart."

"Brian I will be fine, I was tired and pissed at that evil bitch. I didn't answer calls because I needed to cry and sleep. These babies sensed my needs and allowed me several hours of rest, until you decided to shake the house. I know you love me, love us but I let my exhaustion and my emotions win today. I won't go to Dr. Kabre as long as she works for him. I will find another doctor to bring these babies into the world, we have a little time."

"No Sarah, that's just it…….Kim doesn't work for him. She interviewed but she isn't going to get the job. I spoke to Dr. Kabre today, before you ask, it's not because of me. He is looking for a nurse and a technician of which Kim is neither. I don't know what she thought when she came to the office today but she isn't working in our building. I am going to have her banned from the building first thing tomorrow. I will have security alerted and if we need a restraining order, I will get that too. Baby she is never going to be in our lives in any capacity. Can I climb in that bed with you and calm our babies down? My girl needs her sleep you know." Brian pulled his shirt over his head revealing his 8 pack of abs (seriously 8 of them and a gorgeous grin).

"Dear god Brian, how is a girl supposed to refuse that body anything? I could use some cuddle time but a bath would be amazing right now. Why don't we go soak in the tub and I will let you wash my back." Sarah was now leading Brian to the master bath with its large soaking tub.

This new tub was beginning to feel like the best investment ever. Keeping the claw foot tub would have been a great idea, given the age of the house. Keeping it original was the plan but that big soaker tub stole my heart the minute I saw it. I figured I was going to raise my children in the home my grandmother left me so a few upgrades were needed. Now that I see Brian filling that tub so we can enjoy it together solidifies my decision as best idea ever.

"Let me get you in the tub first then I will slide in behind you. I need to make sure my wife is safely seated before I start all my romantic moves." Brian was shooting his sexy grin at Sarah and it was working.

"You can turn down the sexy handsome, I am already smitten with you. Plus I am carrying your babies and I even married you."

"The sexy is natural so I can't control it but I am damn glad you are smitten because I am never letting you go. We let that happen once already when we were kids, I won't let it happen again. We are lifers Sarah and I couldn't be a happier man."

Brian grabbed the big soft sponge and began rubbing circle son Sarah's back. As the sponge made its way to her stomach Sarah cried out. She was grabbing her stomach as she folded forward in pain.

"Oh my god Brian, something doesn't feel right. I have never had any pain before, what is happening?"

Brian jumped out of the tub and grabbed a towel, quickly drying off as he helped Sarah up. He needed to get her to the bed and figure out if this was a cramp or something worse. He no sooner made it to the doorway when Sarah grabbed his hand as she bent over in pain again. That was two very serious pains in less then three minutes. There is no way these babies were ready yet. They had at least 14 weeks before this would be possible.

"Sarah I need you to get to the bed, can I carry you or do you want to walk? I need to check you out before I call your doctor but I need you in bed."

"I want to walk but it hurts so damn much. What's happening Brian? I can't be in labor, it's too soon. Please tell me it's normal and I will be ok!"

"Sweetheart I need you to relax and try breathing slowly. I am going to pick you up and carry you to the bed but I need you to relax. These babies are just testing you but I need to make sure, ok?"

"Yes, ok." Sarah was struggling to speak as another sharp pain hit and she tried to remain upright.

Brian gently scooped Sarah up in his arms like he was cradling her. The few feet they had to travel to the bed seemed effortless for Brian. He gently laid Sarah down and had her lift her knees. With one hand on Sarah's belly and the other hand on his phone, Brian was silently praying that everything was going to be ok.

CHAPTER 27

"Letty what do you mean Tim left before Rose was born? Where the hell did he go? Does he even know he has a daughter? If you are keeping anything from me, now is a good time to fill me in. I am waiting for my bag so I can head to the hotel but I will come to the hospital first if I need to." August was watching the carousal filled with other people's luggage waiting to catch a glimpse of his leather satchel. He should have just carried it with him but checking it in seemed less of a hassle. Now he was surrounded by people who were grabbing bags like it was a Black Friday door buster sale.

When his large satchel finally appeared he shot through the crowd to retrieve it. Letty still hadn't elaborated on what was going on but he knew she was in the room with Amy. Letty wasn't one to be discreet so this was far bigger than a wayward husband issue.

"I am going to ask you questions and I want you to reply with a simple yes or no. This will not require you to leave Amy, can you do that?"

"Yes." Letty's reply was short and all that was needed.

"Has Amy told you why he isn't there?"

"Yes."

"Is he planning on leaving her?"

"Sort of."

"That wasn't one of your options Letty. I need you to stick with the agreed terms of this conversation. Is there another woman?"

"Yes."

"Son of a bitch! I will kill this little bastard! Is Amy ok?"

"Yes."

"Why is she ok? Has this been going on for a while?"

"No."

"Will she take him back when he comes crawling back to her?"

"No."

"Letty you need to walk to the hallway because I am starting to get angry and need more information."

"Yes."

"You can discontinue the one word answers and just get to the hallway."

"Ok, I am in the hallway but I have to whisper. When I arrived I noticed bruising on Amy's arm and her upper thigh. I thought maybe she had had a tough delivery and the marks were part of the whole push thing but the more I looked I realized they were older. I asked her about them but she wouldn't tell me anything. August, he was hitting her! He was hitting her while she was pregnant and before that. She never told me August, she never said anything to me. I didn't know!"

"Letty is Amy ok now? Did the bastard do more than what you saw?"

"No but August she is so broken. I never suspected anything. He was so good at fooling me and Amy was too embarrassed to tell me. She is ready to pack up everything and leave. She can't let him get his hands on Rose, she knows she has to protect her child."

"I will find him and break every bone in his body! I need you to send me her address, I am calling a moving company to pack up and move all her belongings before she gets discharged. Is the lease on the house in her name or both?"

"It's in his name so I am not sure if you can get in. August you can't touch him, I need you. Amy and Rose need you."

Damn it, Letty is right. If I touch a hair on his sorry head he will have me arrested. He should be arrested! What kind of man puts his hands on a woman, a pregnant one at that? If I were a younger version of myself nothing could stop me from righting this wrong!

"August I need to get back into the room but I will text you the address. I need her things delivered to my house, we will figure out what comes next once we are home."

"I will get her things taken care of in the morning. It's too late to reach anyone now but I will be grabbing a rental and heading to the address. Kiss Amy for me and I will be by soon." August ended the call as he climbed the stairs to the rental car office. He was grabbing any car available and getting this all resolved fast, Amy was not going to be dealing with this.

The rental was easy enough to find as there were only three in the lot.

August unlocked the car and heard a ping on his phone followed by another one. When he pulled out his phone he opened Letty's text showing the address he requested. August quickly typed it into the cars navigation system then opened the other message on his phone.

Emma: *I hope you had a nice flight, I am headed to bed soon but wanted to tell you that I miss you already. Call me when you can and enjoy that new baby.*

August: *It was a boring flight but I made it unscathed. I have plenty to do in the little time I will be here. I would love to hear your voice before my head hits the pillow. Can I call you when I get to the hotel? Even if it's just to say goodnight?*

Emma: *I will keep the phone by my bed, no matter the time, call me.*

 August placed his phone in the cup holder and began following the directions to Amy's house. A small part of him wanted Tim to be there but he knew it was best if he wasn't.

After several turns and a few red lights August had arrived at his destination. There were no lights on in the house but a car sat in the driveway. If anyone was here August was going to make sure they were awake.

He parked the rental behind the car in the driveway and approached the front door with purpose. If Tim was here it was going to take epic amounts of self control not to break his nose. August pounded the front door then held the door bell down so it continuously rang. If there was anyone in the house they weren't sleeping now.
Several minutes passed and there was no response from inside the house. August grabbed the door knob and turned the handle, it wasn't even locked.

Once inside August began turning on lights and looking for keys. He would need keys for the moving company and he wasn't going to leave without locking the door. As he headed down the narrow hallway he stopped at a small room that was probably going to be the nursery. Aside from a rocking chair, there were no furnishings, they had nothing ready for the new baby. The second door opened to a bathroom that looked to be the only one in the house. The last door was ajar but it was pitch black inside. August pushed the door and felt for the switch when the smell of smoke hit his nose. Alarmed at the thought of smoke in an empty house he flipped on the light.

Sitting on the bed was a scantily dressed female attempting to light a spoon with an uncooperative lighter. Next to the woman on the bed was a very intoxicated Tim looking as though he was unable to move. Neither occupant even bothered to be concerned that a stranger was in the house.

August saw the keys sitting on a dresser and reached for them when the woman slowly raised her eyes to look at him. Her gaze was hollow, there was no sign of life in her eyes and she had lost any ability to speak.

"I will be taking these keys since neither of you are in any shape to drive. I will be back in the morning with movers to clear this place out. If you are coherent when I return the car keys will be returned. I suggest you get rid of anything illegal as I will be bringing the police with me."
The girls stare turned to a panicked sweep of the room, she nudged her bed partner in an attempt to wake him. He wasn't going to get up any time soon, the smell of alcohol was so thick in the room August's eyes burned.

August left the house and headed to the hotel to check in. Two days should be plenty of time to handle this shit show. Amy was raised so much better than the life she was living. Why had she allowed this man to remain in her life while she carried his baby? He was not the man Amy deserved, hell he wasn't even a man as far as August was concerned. Amy was taking everything worth moving and this low life was going to let her!

CHAPTER 28

The room was nice enough but it wasn't anything he would request again. He had called Letty to see if she wanted him to come to the hospital but Amy was resting, getting sleep for the long day ahead was his new goal. Calling Emma was going to be what got him through the night. In the short time he had known this beautiful, amazing woman, she had become his addiction. Life before Emma was productive, busy and full of success but after? Emma made everything he had accomplished in life pale in comparison. Her presence made his heart ache to be closer, his hands need to touch her, his lips explore her.
Yup, she was the drug and he was the addict.

Reaching for his phone he scrolled through the photos from the little diner. The loving gaze in Emma's eyes made him believe that he was to her, what she meant to him.
Getting lost in the feeling that kissing her left him with and the effect it had on his body was intoxicating. If he heard her sleepy little voice on the phone he may have to take matters into his own hands.

Jeezus, what am I 14?

Scrolling through his phone he tapped on Emma's number,

hearing her voice would help erase the mess he was likely to face in the morning.

The phone was ringing but it was after midnight, the realization that Emma may not answer his call was disheartening.

"August are you ok? How is everyone? I miss you." Emma's sleepy voice had an urgency to it.

Sleepy, concerned Emma. Yeah, I am going to be taking a cold shower before I get any sleep tonight.

"First question, I am fine but missing you more than I ever thought I could. Second question, everyone is fine but I have plenty of work to do tomorrow. I hope to see that new baby around lunchtime, I will send you photos as soon as I do. It's so good to hear your voice Em. I can't help thinking about your messy hair and those beautiful sleepy eyes while talking to you though. I wish I was there with you now but hopefully I can get everything taken care of and head out tomorrow. If Amy is cleared we will be flying back tomorrow evening. I may need to see you as soon as I land." August chuckled as he finished speaking.
This woman cannot possibly understand how much she has taken over my heart. I just can't even imagine leaving her and going back to New York. I could extend my stay, Letty will need me and I could help Amy too.

"August? Are you still there? Are you falling asleep on me?"

Shit! My head can't shut up long enough to hear what Emma said. I need to email Raya and let her know my plans. I am not leaving Emma next week no matter what.

"I am sorry I was deep in thought but I am definitely not sleeping. Sleeping alone tonight is going to suck but I will be looking forward to tomorrow night."
I don't even care that I sound desperate right now, I am desperate. I can't ever remember feeling this way about any woman but Emma isn't just any woman, she is so much more.

"I have to be honest with you August, I have had very little luck falling asleep as well. I am exhausted but I just can't seem to turn my mind off. Part of me thinks we need to talk about everything and the other part wants to live in the now. Take whatever this is at face value and enjoy what we have. I was really enjoying what we had."

Take this at face value? What the hell does that even mean? She can't possibly think this is just, what? What is she thinking this is?

"Emma maybe it's the fact I am wiped out from last night and I mean that in a good way or that I am just exhausted but are you insinuating that what we have is just sex? If I have made you feel that way at all I will gladly let your grandsons kick my ass. Emma please tell me you don't feel that way, that I didn't make you feel that way."

"No! I mean I don't feel that way, you never made me think this thing between us was not special. It's just that everything is happening so fast. Now that there is space between us, it's ok if you need time. I don't want to rush you into anything you're not ready for. I mean we have only known each other a few days

August and I would hate for this to end badly. I mean you have a life in New York, you have a home and a business there. I knew going in, you were only here for a short time but I got swept up in you August and I don't want you to feel pressured into anything."

"Emma at our age rushing into anything isn't a bad thing." August let out a nervous laugh. "I have a life in New York but I am not tied to a desk there. One of the benefits of owning a business is being flexible on the where and how of it all. I get to say where and how Emma and right now that is you. I wish I could say these things to you while I held you in my arms but this can't wait. Emma I want to spend more time with you, I want to see where this goes. I think New York is going to have to wait a little bit because I need more time with you. With Letty, Amy and Rose coming back home I am going to need to get a hotel room. What if I asked you to stay with me?"

"I own a Bed and Breakfast August, you can stay here. There is plenty of room and the kittens think you're comfortable. You could even earn your keep, I have a wedding next week and could use a photographer."

"Already at that phase in our relationship where you use me for my many skills? I would love to document a wedding, who is the lucky couple?"

"Nate and Rachel have decided they cannot wait to be married, so we are having a wedding here. It will be small but I will make sure it's beautiful."

"When I get back consider me your partner then. I have done

my fare share of events, I can help if you would like.”

“I will take you up on that. I wish Rachel’s parents could come, I know she would love for them to be here. Oh and she will be wearing my daughters dress, August she will be a gorgeous bride.”

“Why are her parents not attending? Do they need tickets? A place to stay? Whatever they need I will take care of it, a bride needs her parents.”

“It’s nothing like that, her mother has to have surgery and can’t be traveling. I know Rachel is sad about it but that girl won’t say it. So I need to make sure this is her dream wedding, right here in my garden.”

“Then a dream wedding we will plan, in a week. I will take care of the photographer and the food if that’s ok? I can do that from here while I am missing you.” August was writing down a list of contacts while Emma spoke. He was going to see to it that everything Rachel wanted for her big day was done.

“You really are perfect you know? I have this crazy life and you just jump in feet first with no hesitation. I know I can plan this wedding but I am really excited to have you help me. These kids deserve a beautiful wedding and with your help it’s going to happen. Thank you August. I think I may be swooning just a little bit right now.”

“You only think you’re swooning? What would a guy need to do to get you to actually swoon?” August could feel his eyelids growing heavy but he was not ready to end his call. Talking with Emma like this, relaxed with no pressure was his new second favorite thing to do. Holding Emma while she slept would always be his number one.

In such a short amount of time, this beautiful, strong, independent woman had entered his life and filled every void that existed in his soul. How is that even possible? To be so drawn to a woman that makes everything you have ever known or cared about fade away. To only see, feel and taste her when life continues its chaos around you. I know what I feel for her is more than desire or need but what does that even mean? Can I even think about my future without Emma in it? The answer is no, I don't want a future that is just a continuation of my past. I want of future with Emma in it, with all her crazy, her family, her feline mafia, I want that life.

The big question is, does Emma want that too?

A life with me?

God I hope so because for the first time in my life, I think I am truly happy.

CHAPTER 29

"Sarah baby, I need you to relax. Can you start taking a few deep breaths, in through your nose and release them slowly through your mouth? I am calling Dr. Kabre now but baby, we may need to head to the hospital."

Brian was trying to keep Sarah calm while silently praying she was just experiencing Braxton Hicks. With these little guys struggling for a position in Sarah's tiny frame and the stress of the day inflicted by Kim this was a very real possibility. Brian was not taking any chances with the safety of Sara or their babies. Dr. Kabre could come to them or he was taking Sarah to the hospital, either way they were going to make sure nothing was wrong.

"Brian I think the pain has let up some, bringing my knees up and breathing has helped but I am still scared. What is happening to me? What am I doing wrong?"

Brian was pulling clothes out of the dresser as he was holding the phone to his ear.

"Baby I am pretty sure it's just a false alarm but I am not going to wait to have you checked out. If I can get your doctor here I will have him check you out but if not, I will be taking you in to the hospital. You and these babies are my world and I am too emotional to be a doctor right now."

Brian heard Sarah's doctor on the other end of the phone as he returned to the bed with a long night gown in his hand. Sarah was still wrapped in a towel from the bath but if anyone was going to see his wife, she was going to be clothed.

"Dr. Kabre, Sarah is having severe abdominal cramping and they were coming about three minutes apart. I have her laying in bed now and she is doing a little better but I am still concerned. Can you come by the house and check on her or do you recommend I just get her to the hospital? I am going to be honest with you, I am not dealing with this well."

"Brian I am actually leaving the hospital now. I had a few patients to check on but I can swing by on my way home. If we need to bring her in I can call the hospital from your house. I think I am about five minutes away. Just keep her calm until I can get there."

"I can do that but if you could hurry I would appreciate it." Brian was pacing the floor rubbing his neck, something he did when he was nervous. It was a habit they had all picked up from their grandfather. Mikey likely got it from both he and Nate but all the boys paced and rubbed their necks as if it helped them remain calm.

Stealing glances at Sarah laying peacefully in the bed, Brian watched out the bedroom window for headlights. He would relax when the doctor arrived but not until then. Brian took the moment of calm and ran down the stairs to unlock the door. He would just tell the doctor to come in and head up the stairs. As

Brian started climbing back up the stairs he heard Sarah groan in pain but not nearly as loud as before. Taking the remaining stairs two at a time he was on the bed in seconds rubbing Sarah's belly and whispering soothing words in her ear.

"Brian if this is labor, I can't do it. I will never be able to have these babies, why does it hurt so much? For something so miraculous and beautiful as bringing life into the world, this is some ugly shit." Sarah sounded exhausted and part of Brian wanted to laugh at Sarah's description but he was too worried about the babies.

"Baby you just said bringing life into this world is both miraculous and ugly shit in the same sentence. These babies have no chance of being ugly with you as their mother." Brian could hear Dr. Kabre on the stairs so he stood and yelled from the doorway.

"In here, she just had another one. What do you need me to do?"

"Relax Brian, I can take it from here. Why don't you step outside for a few minutes, get some air and I will check things out. It's very common for multiples to cause a ruckus, there isn't a lot of room in there for them and sometimes they can start a war in there." Dr. Kabre placed a stethoscope on Sarah's stomach as he pushed and poked his way around Sarah's very swollen stomach.

"How has your sleep been as of late Sarah, are you getting enough at night?"

"Actually no, I haven't had much luck getting consistent sleep.

These littles are doing back flips most of the night."

"How has your fluid intake been? Are you getting enough water? Judging from what I am seeing you definitely look dehydrated. Brian mentioned you left work early today. Are you under too much stress?"

"I guess I really haven't been drinking enough water. Today was just a terrible day and with the lack of sleep on top of the stressful day, it all hit me at once. Are the babies ok?"

"The heartbeats are strong and you haven't had any cramping since I got here, both very good signs. I will still want to see you in the morning at my office to run some tests and make sure everything is as it should be. If you don't start taking it easy my dear, you may just find yourself on bed rest. Now I don't want to alarm you, because what you are going through is very common, but it's my job to make sure we take good care of all of you. I am going to let you get some rest but you need to make sure you up your fluid intake, I don't want to put an IV in if I don't have to."

"That's it? Our babies are fine? What if my cramping starts again before I see you? What do I do?"

"Sarah the babies heart rates are good and strong, no distress. You are not dilating, those are all good signs. The cramping you are having is your uterus preparing your body for the birthing process. You will likely have more cramping as this pregnancy progresses, it's normal."

"So the pains are like labor but not actual labor?"

"Well no, labor is actually more intense but you are scheduled for a C-Section so we won't be getting to that point. If by chance your body decides differently we will be discussing your options. For now I need you to rest and get fluids down. I will see both you and Brian in the morning."

Brian was standing by the door when Dr. Kabre turned to leave. He should have figured Brian wasn't going to leave Sarah.

"Brian I am sure you got all that but I want you guys in my office first thing. I will go in early to squeeze you in. Keep her hydrated and calm and I will see you in the morning. Oh and you can call me Brad, we are both working in the same building and I am pretty sure we will be spending a lot of time together." Brad smiled and headed down the stairs.

"Thanks for coming Brad, we will be there first thing." Brian walked to the bed holding a large bottle of water. He removed the lid and handed it to Sarah.

"Drink this and I will rub those feet and legs until you fall asleep. We can talk about work, stress and everything else tomorrow after your appointment. If I get a vote, I pick bed rest until they start kindergarten." Brian kissed Sarah's nose and started the promised foot rub.

This man was everything I had ever hoped to find. The way he loves me with such tenderness and care is all I will ever need. These babies are going to learn how to love completely because of him. Sometimes I want to pinch myself just so I know it's all real, he's real.

CHAPTER 30

"Nate, are you asleep?" Rachel was wide awake and not having much luck shutting down her brain. The baby, the wedding plans, Nate's neck and her parents, were monopolizing her thoughts. Her book was on hold until everything slowed down but her publisher was a softy, when they had heard about everything going on, they offered up the extension.

Once Nate saw the specialist and began therapy everything would be better. Granny was a complete life saver with everything else.

Since there was no answer from Nate, Rachel grabbed a robe and headed for the stairs. Maybe the baby needed a glass of milk and some gooey butter cake, you know… comfort food.

When Rachel reached the bottom stair she noticed the kitchen light shining through the dining room. Not hearing any commotion, Rachel proceeded into the kitchen, where she saw Mikey seated at the table. His head was in his hands as his elbows rested on the table.

"Mikey it's late, what are you doing in here? There better be some butter cake left or you may just get hurt." Rachel nudged Mikey with her hip as she walked to the refrigerator.

"Looks like we both can't sleep tonight. I haven't gotten into the cake but now that you brought it up, grab the forks." Mikey pulled the cake onto the table and started pealing back the foil.

"I am only sharing because you seem down." Rachel filled two glasses with milk and set them on the table and sat down next to him. "What's going on Mikey?"

"This thing with Granny has me all messed up. I mean I get that she needs friends and people to talk to that aren't us. I just can't figure out this guys angle. He doesn't need her money, he is apparently loaded. He doesn't need her company, he is surrounded by models. Why is he trying to get all cozy with Granny? I mean what's his game?" Mikey was pushing a piece of cake back and forth in the pan. Like he thought the butter cake held the same powers as tea leaves and it would reveal all the answers.

"Mikey I don't know a lot about guys or how they play with a woman's heart but I do know Granny. If she felt for a second that August wasn't genuine, she would not be spending time with him." Rachel grabbed the fork out of Mikey's hand and took a large bite out of the piece of cake he was playing with. "I can't let you murder butter cake in my presence Mikey, it's sacrile-gious." Rachel smiled as crumbs fell from her lips.

"I know Granny isn't some gullible woman and can protect herself but why now?" Mikey looked Rachel in the eye with a sadness to his.

"It's been a long time for Granny and I honestly don't know how she made it through. I know she loved your grandfather with everything she had. I don't know what I would do if I ever lost

Nate. When you love someone so completely like that, do you ever really get over it? Maybe with all of you becoming grown ups she realized it was just...... time, you know? I think she deserves love again after what her heart has endured, don't you?"

"When you're not being mean to me, your actually pretty smart." Mikey bumped Rachel's shoulder with his as he began picking at the cake again.

"Mikey even though we just had a moment, I will not hesitate to stab this fork into your hand if you continue to play with that cake!" Rachel slid the pan in front of her as she took a big drink of milk.

"For the record violence is never ok, especially before the sun comes up. Thanks for the chat Rachel but I need sleep." Mikey stood and headed towards the doorway when he noticed Granny standing off to the side.

"Mikey if you could spare an old woman a few minutes I would love to get some air." It wasn't really a question, it was more like an order. Granny walked to the back door and waited for Mikey to join her.

The night air was crisp, summer was fading quickly into an early fall. Granny had been heading to the kitchen for some water when she heard Rachel talking. She had known Mikey was having trouble with her spending time with August but hearing him talk to Rachel pulled at her heart. She should have spoken to the boys before she let herself get all caught up in August. It would have been the right thing to do, if it all hadn't happened so fast. Even though the boys were grown men, she knew they were still her little boys, the ones she had raised.

"Mikey walk with me to the garden, I do love the garden." Granny grabbed Mikey's hand and walked down the stone stairs.

"Granny I want you to know how sorry I am. I just worry about you and we hardly know this guy." Mikey stopped walking so he could face her, he wanted to understand what was going on in her head.

"Mikey, August has been nothing but honorable and caring since the minute I met him. Nothing he has said or done has been out of line. I enjoy spending time with him, more than I ever thought possible. I should have had a conversation with all three of you boys but everything happened so fast. Nate got hurt, then Rachel but not once did August leave my side. I have had more than my share of heartache in this life of mine but you boys were my saving grace." Granny began walking down the moonlit path toward the gazebo. Mikey trailed behind her trying to sort out what he wanted to say before actually saying it.

"I know Granny but I just felt like it was all so fast, too fast. It's like he knocked on the front door and then never left you alone. This isn't like you, none of this is anything like you."

"You were always my sweet, smiling baby boy. So little when we lost your parents, you needed me so much. You would sneak into my room at night just to snuggle before I carried you back to your bed. Your brothers needed me too but differently, they were so much older, stronger. You boys are all grown up now, with lives of your own. Soon you will be starting families, having babies, that I still intend on spoiling but you won't need me all that much. I realized when, August showed up, that maybe I was so focused on my boys that I might have missed out on a small bit of life. Don't misunderstand me, I would do it all again and not change a thing. August just made me feel like I was more than Granny. For the short time I have known him, I learned I didn't have to be strong, I could let someone be strong for me. I haven't had someone lighten that load in a lot of years. I can still take care of myself but my heart loves that you want to too." Granny took a seat in the gazebo and patted the bench for Mikey to join her.

"Granny I don't remember much about them, mom and dad but I remember everything you told me over the years. I only know you, how you kissed my scrapes, made me soup when I was sick. You made every birthday cake just how I liked it and read to me whenever I asked. I feel bad about not remembering them but I would feel worse not having all those memories with you. I don't mean to be this crazy protective freak but I can't help thinking he wants to take you away from me, us. I know it's stupid but I don't know how to share you with someone other than my brothers." Mikey was picking at the chipping paint on the bench afraid to look into Granny's eyes. He knew in his head what he wanted to say but he wasn't sure that what he verbalized matched.

"My dear sweet boy you will never have to share me with anyone. When you want or need me, I will be there. You and I have a special connection that can never be broken. You will always carry a big piece of my heart right there inside you." Granny put her palm on Mikey's chest. "I will always have you and your brothers right here in my heart. Now that you all have wives or soon to be wives and future babies, I have room for them too. August is a sweet man and I don't know what the future holds for us but no matter what that is, you will still have me however or whenever you need me. No one will ever change that sweetheart, no matter what they do."

"I just want what's best for you Granny, we all do."

"Well then we all want the same thing Mikey. I promise not to go off the deep end, if you promise to let me try this whole dating thing."

"I promise to let you try but I can't promise not to care." Mikey gave Granny a weak smile.

"Now that we have all that taken care of, what do you say we head inside for some coffee and a piece of that cake. The sun will be up soon anyway, may as well start the day with sugar and caffeine." Granny stood and looped her arm in Mikey's as they made their way to the house.

Mikey opened the door and noticed Rachel had fallen asleep at the kitchen table. A small chuckle escaped as he walked to the table where Rachel was sleeping.

"Unless you have another cake stashed somewhere it looks like we need to settle on coffee and toast."

Rachel had fallen asleep after finishing off all the butter cake and milk, fork still in hand.

"Well I had an extra cake for Letty but I can pull it out for us. Let me wake this poor girl and send her on up to bed first. She is going to need to sleep that meal off or she is going to be miserable." Granny rubbed on Rachel's shoulders gently to get her attention. When Rachel jerked to life, there were crumbs in her hair and some stuck to her cheek. She began chewing while looking frantically around the kitchen as if she was lost. Rachel had fallen asleep while chewing the last bite of cake. Mikey's laughter brought Nate down the stairs to witness his future wife's predicament. She was definitely a sight and Mikey was enjoying this a little too much.

"Oh this is definitely going on Instagram!" Nate barked out a laugh as he snapped pictures with his phone. The surprised look on Rachel's crumb covered face was well worth the walk down the stairs. Nate knew he was safe from retribution, as long as he was recovering, so he was enjoying this moment more than anyone.

CHAPTER 31

The movers had loaded up the truck with everything that belonged to Amy and headed out. Tim was nowhere to be found but the police were going through the house so it was unlikely he would be back any time soon. August had explained the situation to the local police who were more than happy to help out. Amy was going to be discharged this morning and tickets for their flight home were ready to go. It isn't an ideal situation, taking a newborn on a long flight. August had paid to have a nurse fly with them for Amy's peace of mind. He offered the nurse a return flight and a weeks pay to help Amy with the baby, the nurse was more than happy with the arrangement. August was very ready to hold Emma in his arms again.

"Letty I have a car down stairs ready to take us all to the airport as soon as Amy gets her discharge orders. I have a nurse on standby and ready to fly out with us. The pod of Amy's belongings will be delivered to your house in a couple days. I will have a crew come in and unload it when we are ready. I will be moving to Emma's B&B so that you three have the room to settle in. I have an attorney on retainer who will be handling everything for Amy and Rose. Amy, you and Rose will never have a need that isn't met. I love you like my own so understand, your safety and happiness are all that matters right now."

"Uncle August I can't thank you enough for everything. I am truly sorry I didn't tell you and mom about my situation. I just had so much hope that it would get better. I just thought if he could stop drinking, if maybe he saw Rose he would want to be better. I was stupid for praying for the best in someone when the best had left him a long time ago." Amy was holding Rose in her arms as tears fell on her cheeks. Her life had turned out so differently since Tim had finished school and started his business. She had hoped the stress of running a pharmacy would evaporate as he became more established but it only seemed to get worse. She couldn't love away the monster inside him and she knew that now.

"Sweetheart you were never stupid for loving someone or hoping for better. You have your Uncle and I to help you through this and you will get through this. Rose is a beautiful little girl who will depend on you to raise her to be strong. You are surrounded by people who love you and we will be there even when you don't need us. Now let's get this baby girl ready to meet some pretty amazing people and get you home." Letty was ready to get Amy and Rose back to Colorado and back to where she knew she could be happy. She would settle in, find a new normal and learn to love herself again.

"Amy I have looked over your chart and see you have had no issues thus far. That's good news. You will need a follow up appointment in about six weeks. I see in your chart you will be moving from the area, that's good but make sure to continue your medical care. Rose should be seen by her new pediatrician in about four weeks. Of course if you have questions or concerns you can always call my office. When you choose your new physician we will send your files over, so please have your new doctor get a hold of my office. Do you have any questions for me?" Dr. Schmidt had delivered Rose and had been wonderful with everything. He knew what Amy had been going through and helped as much as she had allowed. Moving away would be the best thing for her given the situation.

"I feel ok, for now, we have a nurse flying out with us to help. I plan to have a new doctor this week and I promise to let you know where to send our files. You have been so great to us, thank you." Amy spoke softly as she waited for her discharge.

"Here is my card, I want all billing for Amy and Rose's care sent to me. I will see to it that everything is taken care of." August was gathering Amy's bags, ready to get on the plane and headed back to Emma.

"Good, I will let the billing department know but please make sure Amy gets follow up care. All the follow up care she needs, I can get you referrals if you'd like." Dr. Schmidt was definitely letting them know he was aware of the situation and wanted Amy cared for. August nodded in agreement and made sure both men understood each other.

Amy was seated in a wheelchair with Rose in her arms as they made their way to the elevators. The hired nurse, Cindy, was pushing the wheelchair and nodded to August with a knowing smile.

He had asked the nurse to purchase the best car seat and supplies for the trip before returning to the hospital. Amy's car was in the parking garage but it wasn't going to make the trip. August offered it to the nurse who was more than happy to take it. The car wasn't much but she had a teenager who would be driving soon and this would help her family out immensely. August was having a new vehicle delivered to Letty's for Amy and Rose that was better suited for them. A new SUV that would keep them safe and provide them the comfort they deserved.

"Cindy, we will meet you at the airport since you will need a car upon your return. I will take my family in the rental and turn it in before we take off. You should find all the paperwork you need in the glovebox but if I forgot anything let me know. You are doing us a huge favor and we are all grateful." August loaded everything into the car and they all made their way to the airport.

"Uncle August, I need to get my things from the house before we leave. Can we just swing by and I will be quick, I promise."

"Amy there is nothing left at your place, I had movers pack up everything and head to Colorado this morning. If there is any-thing that was missed I will replace it but I doubt they forgot anything there. I do not want you worrying about anything, that's what you have us for. Your mother and I will make sure you never have to struggle again. Now relax sweet girl and get some rest, we will be home in no time."

Amy smiled a real smile, the first one in a while. She was safe, Rose was safe and they were going to be ok. Her uncle had been a big part of her life since the day she was born. He looked so much like her dad she would sometimes forget he was gone. August always made her feel like she was loved and could do anything in life. She didn't even see disappointment in eyes when he saw what her life had become. He just came in and took charge, that's who he was. It was a good feeling to know that you are loved no matter how far you fall. Love of family is the purest most fulfilling kind of love and Amy knew she had it, always.

CHAPTER 32

The trip to Brian's building felt like it was taking forever. The babies were active most of the morning but something still felt off. I could not have been more relieved to have Dr. Kabre come over last night. I am still completely freaked about this situation but it did help having the reassurance of my specialist. Now we were going in to his office, confirming we have healthy babies, so I can relax just a tiny bit.

"Sarah I need you to wait in the car while I grab a wheelchair. I don't want you walking any more than you need to until we see Brad." Brian had pulled up to the main entrance of the medical building while he grabbed a chair. The doctor parking was close to the door so it was a little strange that Brian wasn't parking first.

"Brian I can walk from the nearest stall. I came down the stairs just fine this morning. You have to lighten up, you're a doctor for heavens sake."
It was no use in arguing as Brian jumped out of the car and ran inside. The wheelchairs were kept by the main entrance desk for patients. Brian was pushing the chair towards the double doors when Kim walked through them.

"Kim before you even think about speaking you better turn

around and leave. I am not playing your games, I will call security. I know you lied about being employed here and I have no idea why but your game ends now!" Brian was furious at the site of Kim and her fake innocence. He was ready to call in back up if he needed to but Kim was not staying anywhere near his wife.

"Fine Brian, you are right! I am not currently employed here but I am trying to get a job with any of the offices here. I need to be in the medical field Brian, I need this."

"Holy shit! How did I not realize this before? You want to work in the medical office building to find your next victim! Jeezus Kim! You really are pathetic! You cause my wife undo stress, while she carries OUR babies, in the hopes you can land another meal ticket! Rest assured I will advise all the doctors in this building what your plan is. I can guarantee you won't be drawing a check from this building. Do yourself a favor and move on! I have a wife to take care of, you can turn around and leave through the same door you came in," Brian shoved the wheelchair past Kim and headed to the parking area. After he locked the chair in place he ran back to the car, he would park near the chair and Sarah would be safe. When he was just about to the car he saw Kim, she was talking to Sarah! Anger boiled in him as he approached the car where Kim was standing. Just as he was about to unleash his rage he heard Sarah's voice.

"These babies do belong to Brian and I, there is nothing you can do or say to hurt us. You have no claim on my husband and it's pretty clear he holds no fond memories of you. I am not threatened by your presence nor do I value your opinions on our lives. If you choose to stay around here, I can assure you the outcome won't be pleasant. I have the means to protect our family and trust me when I say……you won't EVER win. Now move out of the way, so MY husband can help me into my doctors office, so WE can check on OUR babies!"

Damn! Sarah is a badass and she comes fully loaded at all times. Brian couldn't speak as he watched Kim storm off. Sarah had handled the evil witch on her own and didn't even look upset.

"Sarah I am going to be honest here, that was hot! You handling that bullshit like a boss, has me wishing we could head back home. Are you ok? I am sorry she is being an insane crazy person but damn honey, you are fierce!"

"Brian there is nothing she can say or do to hurt us. She is evil and all that ugly she has inside her, will eat her up one day. I choose to be the bigger person both metaphorically and physically." Sarah rubbed her stomach and smiled. "These babies and I will not be stressed out over your ex-wife or her crazy ass taunts. Now get me in to my doctor so we can check on our tribe."

Brian smiled as he parked and moved the wheelchair to Sarah's side of the car. With a groan Sarah climbed out of the car and into the chair. The ride in was definitely saving her feet the added stress but walking made her feel like she was exercising. With the rate she was putting on weight, she would need to stay busy or end up on one of those reality shows where she never left the bed.

"Oh good, you guys are here early. Let's ride up together and head straight into my office. Glad to see you opted for the ride in." Dr. Kabre was smiling down at Sarah as he walked with them to the elevators. "This exam will be a little more thorough than last night but I think we need to see how the little ones are progressing. Generally in multiples we determine if a steroid will be necessary to help the progression of the lungs. This will help if the babies decide to make an earlier than planned appearance. We should know today if that's a route we need to take."

Brian, Sarah and Brad were already in an exam room when an ultrasound machine was brought in.
"We are just going to take a look at these little ones, then see where we are in the development. I need you to just relax Sarah and let's get some pictures."

Brian's eyes were glued to the screen as he watched his children stretch and kick while pushing at each other. He chuckled softly as one of the twins held her hand to her mouth with the middle finger raised. That was definitely his daughter, a Van-Byrne for sure.

"I already see our daughter picking up your bad habits Brian." Sarah smiled as she stared at the precious little lives she had growing inside her. They were all moving like crazy and not afraid of the camera.

"Looks like we are almost 24 weeks developmentally, things appear to be progressing really well. I think I would still like to get a few steroids administered in the next couple days. It's a precaution we take with a lot of multiples. It improves the lung function for babies that will be pre-term."

"Brad do you think Sarah will go into labor before her scheduled date? What are we looking at in terms of complications?" Brian was standing now as he watched the screen. He understood the risks of early labor and delivering before 27 weeks. If Sarah was to go into labor early these shots could save the babies lives.

"Brian it is all precaution but I think we may see these little ones try for a very early exit. If that should happen, I want to be prepared to give all three the best possible outcome."

Why is no one talking to me? These babies are inside ME for gods sake! I am the one responsible for their safety and seeing to it they are healthy. I want to hold all three of my babies. I want to see them grow into amazing children and be best friends. I want to have big crazy birthday parties and teach them how to ride bikes. I am scared I won't get that chance, both Brian and my doctor are talking like I am not even here.
"Dr. Kabre, I want the shots. I want what is best for these babies and I trust you to want the same. Brian I love you and I know you want that too but you guys need to talk to me. If I need to lay in bed for the rest of this pregnancy I will! I will eat everything you tell me to and nothing I shouldn't. I want to bring three beautiful babies into this world and I want them healthy. If anything is giving you any reason for concern, you need to tell me what I need to do and I will do it. Whatever it takes to make that happen Brian, I will do it."

"Well let's get those shots scheduled but I would like the first one administered today. We will do four shots over the next couple days. I will continue to monitor their development weekly but I am thinking bed rest will be best. I generally want the mother to stay as active as possible but I think we should be cautious. These babies seem a little too eager to make an appearance."

"So we do bed rest until we are full term or should we expect a shorter timeframe? I don't want to pressure you Brad but this is kind of freaking me out!" Brian was trying to remain calm, he was a doctor for gods sake but Sarah and his babies had him forgetting all his medical training.

"Let's all take a deep breath here. I want to get this pregnancy to at least 34 weeks but I have a feeling we could see 27 or 28 weeks realistically. That is early but the longer we keep them inside the better it will be. So we will have to start with bed rest, the only exception will be visits to my office. I want to see you weekly from here on out, possibly twice a week as we progress. There is no reason to be concerned as of yet, so try and relax, both of you. Multiples are notorious for early arrival and I am pretty good at caring for them. So after you leave here I suggest you get everything ready and try to keep Sarah downstairs. She doesn't need to be going up and down stairs for any reason. Are there any questions I failed to answer for you?"

"You answered everything we can think of but I can't promise you I won't call…..a lot! Let's get Sarah ready to go home and I will handle everything else. Thank you for everything Brad, I mean that." The nurse had entered the room with a syringe and pamphlet for Sarah, while Brian made a few phone calls. He was going to have a bedroom downstairs before they got home and then work on the nursery. If these babies wanted to come home early, he was going to make sure they were ready.

CHAPTER 33

"Nate, who are you calling? It's too early to work on wedding stuff and Granny has most of it done already. You better not be working from bed, I need you rested and well for our honeymoon." Rachel had a tray of bacon and eggs for Nate, a large pumpkin muffin for herself. Granny was baking like crazy this morning, Rachel assumed it had to do with August's impending return. She was in the kitchen primped and full of energy before the sun came up this morning. Rachel thought she could grab an early snack then go back to bed but Granny was wired and ready to chat.

"I was just calling the guys at the firehouse, I needed a favor. Sarah is going to be on bed rest, so I called Paul to head over to their house for operation bedroom relocation. Brian wants the bedroom moved to the den and the den furniture moved to the garage. The guys can have it done in about an hour, so Brian is taking Sarah out for breakfast before baby lockdown."

"Oh my gosh, she is going to go crazy on bed rest. Nate we need to help her keep her sanity. She is nowhere near ready to deliver, she has weeks to go. We have to help them, can we get the nursery ready? I feel so bad for Sarah, she is not going to take this well."

"Rachel, baby we will do whatever Brian and Sarah need us to do but we cannot do anything until they need us. Let them get home to the bedroom the guys will be taking care of first. I need to head over there to let them in, if you want to come and make sure I just supervise, you can."

"Yes! I want to help and you are not lifting anything yet. Let me throw on some sweats and I will walk over there with you. How long do we have to make miracles happen?"

"We have about an hour so the sooner we get there, the better. Remember, the guys are headed there now." Nate was throwing on a shirt and heading down the stairs. He moved a little slower but he was still pretty mobile.
"I will let Granny know where we are headed, I will meet you downstairs Rachel."

Thirty six minutes, that's all it took for the five guys to empty the den then move the entire master bedroom downstairs. With Brian keeping Sarah out of the house for another twenty minutes, Rachel had plenty of time to rearrange the room. She wanted the sun to come through the windows and shine on the bed. This would help Sarah rest but not sleep for days on end. Getting sleep is good, especially with babies coming but too much can be depressing. Guys don't understand all the things a woman does, she was happy to bark a few orders of her own.

"Rachel I think the guys are finished with all the heavy stuff so I can send them back to the firehouse. I will stick around just in case we need to move anything. You good with that Nate?" Paul was still feeling guilty over the accident but seeing Nate doing so well made it sting less. He was more than happy to give up a little sleep to help out.

"If drill Sargent Rachel is done barking orders, I think we can all head out. I am not sure Sarah will want an audience when the realization of bed rest hits her. This way Brian can decide if he needs us." Nate had his arm wrapped around Rachel as she examined the room. Rachel was chewing her thumb nail and tilting her head as if she wasn't quite finished.

"Ok, I should probably swing by and talk to Mikey anyway. I um, I found a group that meets weekly and I wanted to thank him." Paul wasn't making direct eye contact as he spoke. He wanted Nate to know he was getting help but he was a little hesitant to share everything.

"Dude, I think that's great! You know I don't blame you right? I should have paid more attention to what was going on but my head was on my woman here and I let my guard down. Before you say anything Rachel, it isn't your fault either. This whole accident helped me realize there is more to life then work. Don't get me wrong, I loved being a badass but now I need to be a badass husband and father. There are things you just don't realize you need until you have them, you know?" Nate kissed the top of Rachel's head as the three of them headed to the door.

"Thanks Nate, I hope I can figure all that out someday but for now I will just keep working on me. I can't get to the us part until I figure out the me part." Paul extended his hand to Nate and nodded at Rachel before heading to his truck. He would see

Mikey then head back to the firehouse to get some sleep before his shift started.

"Well, almost wife, feel like taking a walk around the block before we head home. This fresh air feels good and I could use the exercise. This body doesn't just happen you know, a guy has to sculpt his masterpiece." Nate chuckled as he moved his hand to Rachel's and began walking away from Granny's and toward town.

"Nate are you sure about giving up on the fire fighting? I mean you love it and you are really good at it. I don't want me or our baby to be the reason you give up on your dream. Hell, every little boy's dream is to be a fireman or a policeman and help people or catch all the bad guys. I don't want this to ever be a thing between us, you know? I mean you encouraged me to write, now I have books and stories to tell. It was my dream and you made that jump with me. I just don't want to be THAT wife, the one who forces you to drop your dreams, just so I can have mine."

"I am not dropping my dream Rachel, I am grabbing it with both hands." Nate stopped and placed his hands on Rachel's small stomach and kissed her nose.
"Didn't you hear what I told Paul? There are things that I didn't know I needed until I had them. Until you came into my life Rachel, I didn't know how badly I needed you. Now I can't even picture what my life would be without you. Then when we found out about our little nugget here, I knew I had everything. I don't need to run into burning buildings or be a hero to strangers. I only want to be your hero, our sons hero. I don't need any-

thing else but what's in front of me right now."

Rachel let a small tear escape as she swallowed the lump in her throat. Everything that Nate just said was everything she needed to hear. He didn't know it but Nate became her hero shortly after she pelted him with pizza.

"You know we could have a girl Nate, a girly girl with pigtails and frilly dresses."

"Then it looks like you need to teach me to braid hair, I only know dude stuff. If we have a daughter, I will be the cool dad with painted nails and a kick ass tiara for tea. Now let's go home and help Granny plan our wedding, I gotta smoking hot bride depending on me."

CHAPTER 34

"Paul I could not be happier that you took my advice. These meetings should help a lot. It may not be a cure but with time it should help you turn the corner. I know it's kind of a general group but each person has a demon to tame, you aren't alone." Mikey and Paul were sitting on the patio drinking the tea Granny insisted they have. She had made them an early lunch and enough desserts to feed the entire town.

"I think Granny is trying to fatten us up, does she always go all out for lunch or is today special? If this is an everyday deal you may see me a hell of a lot more."

"I think she is just killing time until Letty gets back, well Letty, Amy and……. August. That guy hasn't left her alone since the day he came to town."

"That's the guy from the hospital right? He seems like a really nice guy but I don't think I had ever met him before that day. When he brought Rachel to the hospital, he was asking questions and even caught her before she fell when she passed out. Here are all of us guys standing around worried about Nate and he just caught her like it was nothing. Then he brought Granny back and he never left her side the whole time. He was just holding her, not trying to talk to her or put any moves on her, dude, he just sat with her. He seems like a solid guy to me."

A car door slammed as Mikey was prepared to respond to Paul. Within seconds August was walking up the driveway with a bag in his hand. The car he exited pulled out and drove off towards town. Why was August here with a bag? Why did the car that brought him leave? I need to get inside and find out what the hell is going on and fast.

"Well Paul, it was great talking with you, I should probably head back inside now. You want to swing by tomorrow, after your meeting, we could talk some more?"

"Yeah that sounds great, thanks. I mean it man, I really appreciate everything. My meeting is at 6:00 so maybe 7:30 or so, is that cool?"

"Yeah, you can eat dinner with us. I am sure Granny will have a feast fit for a king anyway."

"Then I am definitely in, she can really cook and it sure beats the hell out of the firehouse food. I will see you tomorrow, thanks man." Paul nodded at the table as if to ask if he could help clean up but Mikey waived him off. He could clean up and take everything into the kitchen, he was dreading his talk with August and this would hopefully be a distraction.

"Hey Granny I brought in the stuff from the..........son of a bitch! Get your hands off my grandmother! Why am I the only one who walks in on this stuff? Are you two trying to kill me, you know it's killing me right? August please remove your hand from Granny's ass, please God strike me blind!"

"Mikey stop being so dramatic, I have caught you doing far worse. Remember your junior prom and that lovely Anderson girl? What was her name…. Milli, Melli? Anyway, I didn't freak out and I saw things I hadn't seen since your potty training days."

"Oh god Granny stop, I get it! I just wasn't prepared to see all the hands and tongues and…….shit! Can we just not do those things in the kitchen? It's sacred in here, like the alter at church…….. just don't."

"Mikey, it's good to see you again. I think you and I are overdue for that chat, don't you?" August was standing beside Granny with his arm around her waist.

Mikey sighed and nodded his head like a scolded child. He knew he had to have a conversation with August but he had hoped his talk with Granny would make it easier, it hadn't.

"You two will have plenty of time to chat August since you are staying here. Mikey you have a patient coming in today around two, so that only gives you half an hour to help me get August settled. He has another suitcase in his SUV out front, can you grab it for me?"

"Sure……wait, what? He is staying here? I thought he was staying at Letty's for the next eight days, not that I am counting."

"I am right here" August waived his hand in the air "I am giving Amy and her sweet baby Rose space to settle in. Emma was sweet enough to save me from a hotel stay by offering a room. I can grab my bag later if you have things to do, it isn't a big deal.

I will be here for a few extra days, my schedule is clear for the next few weeks. That's not a problem is it?"

"Oh August that is wonderful news! Are you sure you don't have to go back?"

Seeing the glow on Granny's face was enough for Mikey to realize what an ass he had become. Granny deserved to be happy, the look on her face said it all. August made her happy and when he eventually went back to New York he and his brothers would fix her broken heart. She just looked too happy in this moment for Mikey to not to give her his blessing. Damn it!
"I am just going to head to my office and get ready for my next patient. Oh and Granny? I invited Paul to dinner tomorrow, he should be here around 7:30."

"Oh how wonderful, we will have Letty, Amy and Rose here too. I should let Brian and Nate know. We can go over Nate and Rachel's wedding plans since Saturday is fast approaching. Have a great rest of the day Mikey, I love you." Granny was walking with August toward the stairs. There were baby gates on every doorway now, they were meant to keep the kittens contained but it was more like an obstacle course than a deterrent.

"Sorry about all the gates but these kittens are starting to get a little bolder. I figure if I can slow them down Mikey will have a fighting chance." Emma laughed as she stepped over the gate at the bottom of the stairs.

"Hey Granny what's going on?" Nate and Rachel were heading down the stairs holding two very energetic kittens. "Caught these two under the bed, pretty sure the rest of this crew is in the den but I strongly suggest you proceed with caution. For some reason they seem to love ankles." Nate was holding Cleo out in front of him as a precaution.

"August will be taking the room at the end of the hall. Letty and Amy will be getting Rose settled in so I offered to let August stay here. We will be having a big dinner tomorrow so I hope you kids plan on sticking around. You need to be taking it easy Nate, until your doctor says otherwise."

"Yes ma'am, we will be here. August, I guess we will see you around." Nate nodded his head as he made his way over the baby gate to head to the den. Rachel followed Nate's lead with a very unhappy Jac. If these kittens were any indication of what a toddler can do, Rachel was thinking of upping her time at the gym.

"We should call Brian and fill him in on the newest house guest and about dinner. If Sarah is on bed rest, she can still come for dinner, right?" Rachel asked as she placed Jac on the small hammock in the den.

"I think so but I will ask Brian when I call him."

"Good, I want to talk to Sarah about starting a blog. If she is going to be home under strict orders I think it will be a fun distraction. Lots of women are doing them now, documenting her journey could be so interesting. Don't you think?"

"If Sarah wants to blob or whatever then I am sure she will have fun with it. Feel like going to the gym for some leg work? I promise to take it easy." Nate crossed his heart with his index finger.

"Sure but you only get to watch, still not cleared to workout yet and I follow rules." Rachel slapped Nate on the butt as she headed for the door. This was going to be a long few days.

CHAPTER 35

"If this is too rushed Emma, I can go to a hotel, I don't want to overstep. Being so close to you, while you sleep, may drive me crazy. I will want to hold you in my arms and wake up to you in my bed." August stopped unpacking and sat on the edge of the bed.

"August I want you to know that I feel the same way. It's hard for me to imagine life when you leave, go back to New York. I knew going into this, you were only here for a couple weeks. I tried to prepare my heart for that, the end of us. I am afraid I may not have it in me to put the pieces back together. I will break August but I won't regret a minute of us, what we've shared."

August pulled Emma onto his lap and placed a kiss on her lips. His plans were to help Emma and stay for the wedding but the more he stayed, the more he knew he couldn't leave. She was right though, how could he have his work in New York and his heart in Colorado? It wasn't just Emma's heart that would break.

"I have always loved New York and the life it breathes into me. Working where I do, with the people I do, it is amazing. I just don't know if that life is what I need any more. I had a taste of something that I never thought I wanted and now I am questioning everything. Emma I don't know what the answer is, to all these questions in my head but when I hold you, none of them matter. Nothing else matters but what we have, I am so addicted to you it both scares the shit out of me and gives me hope, hope of more."

"I want you to stay here as long as you'd like but I won't be the woman who forces you to choose. I will take everything that you give me and be grateful for all of it. This time with you is what I will remember and how you make my heart feel. Let's not talk about the after yet, you know ……..that after you leave part. We can enjoy what time we have left like there isn't an after."

Emma is unlike any woman I have ever known, the thought of going back to New York without her is killing me. I know her life is here, her family and friends but the selfish me wants her to go with me. Is it selfish to want her to leave everything she loves and come with me? I think we have been alone for so long that we deserve to see where this could go, what it could be. Emma in my world, God that sounds amazing. Taking her to all the places she has never been. Showing her the life that pulses through the city. Even though everything that is New York isn't Emma, I could see her there with me, I could see us.

"Emma, what if you came to New York with me, just a few days? We could go after the wedding and spend a few days, just us? I know your family needs you but I would love to show you my world. Will you think about it?" August began kissing down Emma's neck as he gently caressed her back. Thinking about the alone time they could have in New York made his kisses more urgent, as if they could make her agreeable.

"I have so much happening right now with weddings and babies, I don't think I could just leave. It sounds amazing but that big city life isn't me, I am smart enough to know it's you though." Emma began running her fingers through August's hair as she studied his expression. He looked wounded but deep down she knew he needed his life, his work. Taking him away from everything that made him who he was would be wrong, selfish. She had never been a selfish woman and couldn't start now.

"Let me help you unpack and then we can discuss the wedding. I will feed you an amazing dinner and then we will enjoy the fall sky together from the garden. If we keep talking about you leaving I am afraid I may not be great company." Emma stood and held out her hand to help August up.

"Do you always help and take care of others? When will it be time for you to be taken care of? You deserve to be taken care of, have someone there for you." August gripped Emma's hand tight to his chest and pulled her to him.

"August I honestly don't know any other way. Being strong and taking care of others is more instinct than choice. When your life breaks apart you can let the sadness overwhelm you or you can choose to bury it deep inside. I had too much to lose if I let life's setbacks consume me. My boys saved me in so many ways over the years and taking care of them was part of that. I will never regret any choices I have made or sacrifices it took to get here. Everything I did put me right here and I am so grateful for what I have. Now unpack, eat, then garden, what do you say?"

"I say that demanding Emma may just be my second favorite, first will always be the one I am holding in my arms."

"You can turn down the charm city boy, I still like you a little bit." Emma winked as she headed out the door. She needed space and focusing on dinner was going to help with that.

Going to New York with August, that is just crazy. I have so many people who depend on me, here. I can't just run off all doe eyed, for what? A few days of crazy, unplanned adventures like some college kid. My days of carefree adventure have long since passed. I need to help Brian and Sarah, they will need me. Nate and Rachel, his therapy has only just started, I can't leave him. Mikey, my sweet little Mikey still needs me the most. I just can't push life aside to, to what……..live a little? Enjoy alone time with an amazingly handsome man. One who kisses like he could devour me if I let him. A man who has the ability to make me lose all focus just by looking at me. His smolder is crippling and I am not even sure he knows he is doing it. If he even looks at me I want to do things to him that I have never done before. It's as if he can hypnotize me with just one look.

"Granny I think something is burning, you have anything in the oven?"

"Oh my goodness Mikey, open the windows! I just burned the darn biscuits!"

"You ok? I don't remember you burning anything, ever. Is something wrong, you look flushed."

"Um no, I am fine, it was the dang smolder!"

"The what? What did you say? Smolder?"

Oh my god! I just said smolder, now I have to lie to my grandson!
Church is going to be a long one come Sunday, heaven help me.
August brain, I have August smolder on the brain!
"No honey, the timer, I said the timer is messed up. It's ok, I can
throw in another batch for dinner. Thank you for your help
Mikey, I can take it from here."

August Wander what are you doing to me?

CHAPTER 36

The bridal march began to play, I focused on the aisle that was scattered with rose petals. I needed to focus on something while I waited for Rachel or I was going to lose my shit. I was going to be a husband to the most perfect woman I had ever known in just a few minutes. I had to focus on something or I knew I was going to cry thinking about her. Granny insisted on petals and a white lace runner for Rachel to make her appearance, so yeah, I focused on the petals.

The family dinner we had, was more of a brainstorming session, that had the girls going crazy and the guys agreeing to anything.

August had arranged for the cake, caterer and a photographer since Rachel wanted him to walk her down the aisle. She was going to walk alone since her parents couldn't make it but Granny insisted she have someone walk her down the aisle. August was the only guy at the table who wasn't already in the wedding so Rachel begged him to stand in for her dad.

Looking out at the people who gathered here for us I am reminded that family doesn't need to be blood, it's what's in your heart. I could see Granny smiling in the front row, she had her iPad in hand, probably recording everything going on in front of her. I heard the music start and brought my eyes up to wait on my bride.

Rachel appeared in the large white arch and I felt the air leave my lungs. She was the most beautiful woman I had ever seen and she was mine, all mine. There was a soft glow of sunset behind her making her seem ethereal, breathtaking. I knew I was a lucky man when she agreed to be my wife but here, right now? There were no words to describe what was happening to my heart. I didn't feel the tears fall but realized the wetness on my cheeks when Brian handed me his handkerchief. My eyes couldn't pull away from the vision before me.
Never in my wildest dreams had this been part of my future, someone so perfect in every way.

August was by Rachel's side but I hadn't noticed him walking with her. He had one arm looped with Rachel's the other was holding another iPad. It was then I noticed there was a face on the iPad, Rachel's father. August was walking Rachel down the aisle but he had arranged it so her father could give her away.

I stole a quick glance back at Granny and noticed her iPad wasn't recording it was holding Rachel's mom. Thanks to Granny and August, Rachel had her parents here. I had felt some guilt in going forward with the wedding so soon but I couldn't help being selfish where Rachel was concerned.
Now, in front of everyone we loved, we were becoming husband and wife. Our two lives were now going to be one, we were going to be one. Nothing in life has ever given me so much to be thankful for until this moment, the moment that Rachel's hand was placed in mine.

August and Rachel's dad handed me this beautiful, smart, crazy, amazing woman to finish walking down the aisle. I had hoped to get my emotions under control before we exchanged our vows but the thought of being minutes away from your forever……yeah, it was too much.

I stood facing Nate, looking into his eyes, seeing the love he had for me trail down his cheeks. I knew in that moment pelting him with pizza was the perfect beginning to our story.
This man saw me at my worst and loved me anyway. He never expected anything more than what I was willing to give him and he loved me anyway. This big, strong, handsome man was mine to have for eternity. The tears we were crying today (yes we, I am a blubbering mess) proved we were meant to be together. The amount of love we have for each other, kept our hearts full and made our eyes leak. Nate is my once in a life time love, my fairytale. The one that every little girls dreams of and he was all mine.

August took his seat next to Emma and placed both iPads in the stands he had built. Rachel's parents were every bit a part of this wedding as they all were.

Emma was so focused on the young couple exchanging vows that she didn't even notice August was holding her hand.

Emma was stunning, the look in her eyes as she watched Rachel and Nate exchange vows brought a tear to my eye. The complete love and adoration she held for these kids, all of them, was overwhelming. Emma was the one woman who could make you lose all focus and fall completely in love. You heard that right, in love.

CHAPTER 37

"Brian, it's Detective Ray down at the police department. I need to see if Sarah can come in and help us out with a line up. We have a suspect in custody that we believe is linked to the robbery and assault on her a few months back. If we could get her to look at a line up it would help us out. We recovered some of her personal belongings as well so it's a solid case if we can get her to ID the suspect."

After all this time they finally have something? Sarah isn't leaving her bed, there is too much risk involved. My wife and babies are not going to be subjected to anything that could harm them. "Detective, my wife is on bed rest and cannot endure stress of any kind. I am grateful you caught the guy but there has to be another way. I cannot allow my wife to jeopardize her health or that of our children to come down for a line up. Can we do this any other way? Maybe through photographs or virtually? We need this guy held accountable but I need my wife and children safe."

"Let me send over a few photos and you can have Sarah call me back. It's important that she be the one to identify the attacker. When this case goes to court I don't want any loopholes."

"Absolutely. I will speak with Sarah now, can you send over the photos?"

"I have six photos coming over now. I need her on the phone as she looks them over. Brian, I may need you to come in as I have some details that might concern you."

What could I possibly add to this investigation? I was the treating physician, there were no additional details from that night I didn't turn over. Sarah wasn't even conscious when she came in that night. She was so small and helpless when I first saw her on that gurney. The kind of savage that could hurt someone like her makes me want to hunt him down myself.

"Got it, I will have Sarah call you but detective I am not sure what help I can be. Once Sarah looks through the photos, I will come down if you still need me to."

Brian headed to the den where Sarah was resting comfortably on their big bed. The wedding yesterday had taken a lot out of her but she was determined to enjoy normal for just a couple hours. Her doctor had agreed to let her go if she sat the whole time and went straight to bed after. Sarah was relieved she could actually put on clothes and be around people. It wasn't that she was in isolation or anything but to enjoy a stress free outing, yeah it was welcomed. The longer she was able to keep these babies from coming into the world too soon, the better.

"Baby I really hate to bother you when you are looking so relaxed but that call was Detective Ray from downtown. They have some leads in your assault case. He would like you to call him while you go through some photos he sent over. You think you can do this now or would you rather wait? I am ok with whatever you decide, you and these babies are more important right now."

"Brian I am fine, I have rested and could use a distraction right now. Let me see the phone and the pictures please. I just feel bad for this guy, he was clearly down on his luck and desperate."

Brian handed Sarah the laptop with the emailed photos as well as the phone. Sarah didn't hesitate to hit the call back number as she opened the attachment. Her strength and determination was amazing. Brian saw Sarah's eyes grow large as she inhaled.

"Sarah, baby what is it? Did you see him, the guy from that night?"

Sarah looked up at Brian, nodded her head as she spoke into the phone.
"It's him, number three, I remember the look in his eyes like it was last night. I thought he was homeless and needed food. Why did he do this?"

"Mrs. VanByrne, Sarah, he isn't from here and he isn't homeless from what we can tell. We found items that belong to you in his car and a few other things linking him to Seattle. I need you to be absolutely certain this is the guy."

"I am 100% certain it's him. Should I be worried? I mean he hasn't bothered me since that night. I am ok, right?"

"You can rest assured we won't be letting him out any time soon. Can I speak with your husband now? I need to ask him some questions about a few details that have come to light."
"Yes, absolutely. Thank you so much for catching him, I am

glad he is off the streets." Sarah handed Brian the phone and laid her head back on the pillow. Her shoulders sagged as a sigh of relief escaped. The guy that attacked her was off the streets and she and her babies were safe. Even though she hadn't let the incident consume her, it was always present in the back of her mind.

Brian kissed her head as he headed to the kitchen speaking softly into the phone as he walked.

"What do you mean there were items in his car that I should know about? I do not know this guy or what he has to do with me or my wife. What could possibly be so concerning that I would need to come down there?" Brian was pacing in the kitchen looking for anything to help him make sense of all this.

"We found a hotel key in the suspects car. We assumed he was staying there but when we questioned the desk clerk..........the room was rented and paid for by a Kim VanByrne. Brian I know that's your ex-wife but whatever ties she has to this guy and why he attacked Sarah are not adding up. Did you know Sarah before the attack?"

Oh god, this is not making any sense. Why would Kim be connected to a guy that attacked Sarah? I didn't meet her, again, until that night. This all feels like a bad dream.

"Detective, we knew each other as kids but I swear to you that night was the first time I had seen her as an adult. I didn't even know it was my long lost girlfriend until days later. This is all so crazy I don't know where to begin."

"I am going to be honest here Brian, this may be a lot bigger than a simple robbery. We haven't been able to locate Kim for questioning but I think we should keep a car outside your house as a precaution. Until we know more it would be best if you and your wife used extreme caution. I am not sure this guy is the only one you need to worry about."

Surely this is a mistake. Why would Kim go to all this trouble, we're divorced? She moved on long before I did, why Sarah? I didn't even know Sarah when the attack happened. Could she have known about the babies?
Oh god!
What if she got the letter before I did about the sperm donation? It was anonymous, there is no way she could have tied that to Sarah, is there?

"Detective, I think you need to know that Sarah was carrying my babies when she was attacked. Before you ask, I didn't know anything about it. I had donated my sperm in Seattle when Kim and I divorced. I only found out that Sarah was the recipient after we started dating. There is no way Kim would have known these details, is there?"

"I need you to send me any information you have on the clinic and the doctor involved. I don't want to close out this investigation until we have all the details. Brian is there a reason she would want to interfere with the birth of your children?"

Son of a bitch!
Kim has been causing Sarah stress intentionally this whole time. What would she gain from it all? She lost me a long time ago but then she never really had me. Why would she want

Sarah to lose the babies?

"I don't have any answers, I don't know why she would do this. I know she is here, in town. She was trying to get a job in my building, we ran into her a couple times. She knows I am married to Sarah and that we know the babies are mine. I would have never thought she was capable of anything like this. I don't even know what her end game could possibly be."

"Send me the paperwork you have and we will go from there. Brian don't let your guard down until we have her in here for questioning. The car should be outside now and I will make sure we have 24 hour coverage. I will let you know if we get any updates or if we need anything else from you."

Brian ended the call as he returned to the den. Sarah was sleeping peacefully as the sun peaked in the window. The car detail was parked on the street as promised. What would possess a woman to become so insane? There is no way I am going to work and leave Sarah home alone. I can get my partner to cover my patients until this all goes away. It will go away, won't it? Sarah and our babies need it to all go away soon.

Brian climbed onto the bed and pulled Sarah to him. "I love you so much baby, I will protect you with everything I have."

CHAPTER 38

"August thank you for everything, you made the wedding so much more than I could have hoped for. Everything was so beautiful, having Rachel's parents there the way you did, was so thoughtful. You are every bit the man I knew you were and I will miss you so much." Emma was curled up in August's arms as they sat on the patio looking out at the garden.

The service August had brought in, set up and cleared out every bit of wedding décor. The cake was a beautiful tower of roses and silver filled with the most delicious raspberry purée, again August. The pictures were handled by his intern from New York, whom August assured me, was as spectacular as he was. There was not much I needed to do except get Rachel ready. Her hair and make up were even gifts from August, every bride should be pampered on her special day, his words. This man was everything I needed him to be at every point in my life right now but he was leaving.

He had gotten a call from his assistant this morning about a shoot he had to take. He would be leaving first thing tomorrow for his life in New York. He had asked me again to join him but I couldn't leave now. I agreed to help Mikey in the office until Amy was ready to start. I had Mikey and Gabby's wedding coming up in a few weeks and Brian's babies would be here before you know it. Life would be back to normal and I would need to figure out what that meant for me and my heart. I always knew August would leave but I hadn't thought about how much it was going to hurt.

"Emma please don't cry, we have tonight and I don't want to see hurt in your beautiful eyes for the little time we have left. I will be coming back once I get this job out of the way, I can't stay away from you." August kissed the top of Emma's head as he pulled her tight against him. How was he going to leave and not feel his heart break away in the process?

"Give me these few tears and I promise I will be better for our remaining time together. I just need my heart to weep a little so I don't crumble to bits later. I would much rather you kiss these tears away then cry alone after you leave."

"Emma I wish you were coming with me but I understand your obligations. Why did we wait so long to find each other? There were so many times over the past 20 years that I should have met you but never once crossed your path. I feel cheated by the universe, I should have been given this, with you, a long time ago. I hate that I didn't know you sooner."

"I wasn't ready for you sooner August. I needed my heart to heal, willing to beat again, before I could make room for you. You helped me find me again and I am so grateful to the universe for bringing you here. There are always positives in every situation, I am choosing to focus on those."

I wasn't ready for anyone until this beautiful man showed up at my front door. I felt my walls crumble the minute his eyes met mine. I knew he was going to own me if I let him in, I let him in anyway. I knew our time together was going to be short but I let him in anyway, ignoring the expiration date. The worst part, my heart will break into a million pieces the minute he boards that plane. My life is no match for the draws of New York, I would be a fool to think otherwise.

"Ummm Granny, I hate to bother you but you have a phone call. I didn't ask who it was but they said it was important." Mikey was standing at the edge of the patio with the house phone in his hand.

"Thank you dear, I will just head inside for a minute August. I will be right back so we can count the stars." Emma winked at August and walked into the house with the phone leaving Mikey on the patio.

"Mikey, why don't you and I have a chat until Emma returns?" August stood and faced Mikey waiting for a reply.

Mikey nodded and walked over to where August was standing. "Look I know you like Granny and it's clear she feels the same way. The thing is, you are leaving for New York and someone has to be here to pick up the pieces. I know I was little when Gramps died but I remember how Granny fell apart. I used to sneak in her room at night so I could stop her tears. She never cried in front of us but at night, she would fall apart. I don't think I can help repair the damage you make when you leave and it pisses me off. She is the strongest person I know……until she isn't. I just want you to know what you will do to her when you leave."

"My plan is to come back as often as I can. I have strong feelings for her and even if you don't believe me, I need her too."

"Visit often? You think that's going to make this better? Every goodbye will crush her, every phone call will keep her clinging to hope. She isn't like the women you are used to, the ones who can just move on. Granny has only ever loved one man and he died! He died August! She doesn't know how to keep her heart from breaking because she has never had to. Now you think you can head back to your life and have everything go back to normal. There is no normal for her, don't you get it? She isn't strong enough to survive this a second time. You may not be dying August but you leaving her, will kill her." Mikey turned and walked into the house as Emma made her way outside.

"Well you two sure look like someone stole Christmas. Is everything ok?"

"Everything is fine Emma, come sit with me and enjoy the stars." August held out his arms and Emma folded into them without hesitation. Holding her close was all he needed right now.

"August, stay with me tonight, in my room. We only have tonight before you fly off to New York and I want to be with you one last time." Emma was talking so softly August almost didn't hear her.

Emma knew exactly what to say and when to say it. I was not looking forward to my return to New York before, now I loathe the idea of it. I don't want to leave, I want to stay right here like this for the rest of my life.

"I will hold you for as long as you let me."

"Careful city boy, you shouldn't make promises you can't keep." Emma laid her head on August's chest and released a painful sigh. If she kept calling him city boy it would remind her heart, he wasn't meant for this sleepy little town that she loved so much.

CHAPTER 39

"I called Emma mom, she said she will be happy to help with RJ. I can start helping Mikey at the office next week, I will stop by to check out his office in the morning." Amy was walking back and forth while patting her daughters back.

"Rose is such a beautiful name, why do you insist on calling her RJ?" Letty handed Amy a fresh burp cloth and rubbed Rose's back.

"She looks like an RJ and I think it will help her become a strong woman."

Letty looked up from the baby and saw the hurt in Amy's eyes. Her daughter had always been strong and independent. When she met Tim in college she began to change. She was still Amy but she wasn't as outgoing as she had once been. Letty assumed it all had to do with college and classes, she was wrong. Amy only went to college for two years before leaving to go to work full time. Tim was working on his doctorate but with Amy earning their livelihood, he could focus on completing his courses sooner. He had told her it was better this way and it was going to provide them a great future. It seems he was full of a lot of big dreams and really big lies.

"We have to get a hold of Nate in the morning to say our goodbyes to August then get a crew over here to finally help us empty that pod that delivered last week. I know it isn't going to be easy sweetheart but if we have lots of help we won't have time to think about it."

"I know mom and I want to be happy about it, I do but part of me is clinging to hope."

"You did the right thing Amy, Rose will be surrounded by love and family, not necessarily blood family but family just the same. You grew up in this town, it's just so perfect to raise children here. So many wonderful people and places to go, it's going to be great."

"I know, it's just going to take time. I promise I will get there mom, I have a perfect little girl depending on me. I think I will take RJ out for a walk before it gets too chilly. I love looking at the night sky here, it's so full of stars, so peaceful. We will just circle the block, don't worry I will have my phone."

"I will head to the kitchen and clean up then, don't be long Rose needs a routine."
Amy smiled as she bundled Rose up in her new stroller, compliments of Uncle August and her soft blanket from Granny. Taking in the night sky was the perfect way to release thoughts into the universe. I needed plenty of thought time, reflection and just peace. I was still pretty sore from everything that happened but I would heal in time, I always healed with time, physically.

I never understood what about me suddenly set Tim off. I worked all day while he attended classes, I cooked for us and took care of the house. I never complained because I knew we had a plan. I couldn't wait to get back to classes and complete my degree but things started to change.
He was coming home later than normal and never wanted to eat. Then he was drinking more and getting irritated at every little thing. When I had discovered I was pregnant I was afraid to tell him, it wasn't part of our plan. When I did finally tell him he seemed happy, it didn't take long to figure out why. He had me trapped and under his control.

Even though Rose was not exactly planned, I couldn't be happier to be her mom. I hadn't put Tim's name on her birth certificate, I left it blank. He didn't deserve to be recognized as anyone's father and I didn't want him to touch her.

"Excuse me but I think you dropped your keys. I didn't want to interrupt you, you were pretty deep in thought but I figured following you any longer would seem creepy. I am Paul by the way, I think we met at Granny's the other night. You are Letty's daughter, right? I think you look a lot liked her. If you aren't Letty's daughter I just made this very weird." Paul was dressed in his uniform, he was on his way to the firehouse, when he saw Amy walking. He stared a little too long when he saw the keys fall onto the sidewalk but noticed Amy had just kept walking. She was clearly distracted and it looked like she may even have been talking to the sky.

"Sorry, yes I am Letty's daughter Amy and we did meet at

Granny's, this little peanut is Rose Jewel, RJ for short. She was sleeping when we were at dinner. Thank you for finding my keys, I have a lot on my mind and wasn't really paying attention. You work at the firehouse with Nate, right? My mom and I were going to call him about getting some of you guys over to help me unpack a pretty big pod in the morning."

"I do work with Nate and I can get the guys together to help. They actually like the exercise and it's a nice change from the gym. Just name a time and place and I will make sure we are there." Paul was really intrigued by Amy. She was so small and timid but beautiful, yeah she was beautiful. Paul hadn't noticed a ring on her finger at dinner but he hadn't had a chance to speak to her either.
"Oh my gosh, that is so good of you. I am staying at my moms house and the pod is in the driveway. I didn't pack it up, Uncle August had it done, so I am not sure what we are up against. I will be happy to pay you and provide a great breakfast for you all to show my appreciation. It will help me out a ton."

"We will be happy to eat but you are not paying us, this is what friends do."

"Well thank you so much, will 7:00am be too early? I can actually make any time work if it isn't a good time." Amy was rocking the stroller back and forth, not that Rose was fussy it was more to calm her own nerves.

"We will be there bright and early but I am going to warn you, the guys can eat."

"Perfect, I can cook a mean breakfast. I guess I will see you in the morning then."

"See you in the morning Amy. I am glad I got you see you tonight but maybe put your keys someplace safe." Paul handed Amy her keys and headed toward the firehouse.

Amy looked up at the stars and gave them a thankful nod. It was kind of nice having a simple conversation with a man and not worrying about where his fist was going to land. This was going to be ok, she was going to be ok.....eventually.

CHAPTER 40

"August, it's time to wake up. If you don't get moving you are going to miss your flight." Emma was laying next to August in her bed, trying desperately not to break apart. It was her last few hours with him and she was determined not to cry. In just the few weeks she had known him, she had fallen hard. This was going to be unbearable after his plane took off but she would be ok. They could talk on the phone or text after he landed. That would be enough, wouldn't it?

"You are the most beautiful sight to wake up to Emma, I don't want to get out of this bed. Before you say anything, I know I have to but I just love being here, with you."

Emma smiled a sweet smile and slowly climbed out of bed. She needed to get in the shower before the tears started to fall. If she released them in the shower they didn't count as tears, right? "I am just going to take a quick shower before we head out but you are going to have to get out of that bed city boy."

"If that's an invitation, I will be happy to get out of this bed and join you." August sat up grinning, hoping to have just a few more private moments with her. Another memory he could take with him, when he returned to New York.... alone.

"August every part of me wants to say yes but I need this small separation to prepare my heart. I will be quick I promise, then we can spend the rest of the time we have left together." Emma walked into the adjoining bathroom and gently closed the door before her first tear fell. With blurry eyes she turned on the shower then stepped in, before her flood of tears could mix with the water, she heard the door open.

"I can't let you cry alone Emma, my heart hurts for us too. Let me hold you in private one last time before I have to leave, please." When Emma raised her face to look at August it was like a knife had pierced his heart. Her eyes were not shining with the light he had loved but looked more hollow and pained. August quickly climbed into the shower and grabbed Emma, pulling her to him, as his lips captured hers. Even when she tried to turn her face to hide her tears he held her face firmly in place.

"Don't turn away from me Emma, I can't stand that I am the cause of this hurt. You have to know holding you or even just being in your presence, breathes life into my soul. I don't know what the future holds for us but you have to know that you are the reason I finally have hope. Hope that life has so much more to offer than what I have seen in my many years. I am a changed man Emma and you are the reason for that, you make me want more."

"August you have given me so much to be thankful for in these last few weeks. I feel alive again, on the inside and I have you to thank for that. Part of me wishes you weren't leaving but I know you have to go back to your life. I will never regret anything we shared no matter how much it hurts my heart. You are an amazing, caring man August." Emma's voice broke as the uncontrolled sobs broke free. "I am going to miss you so much."

August wrapped his arms around Emma's small frame and let the water from the shower carry her tears down her body. Leaving her was a mistake he could feel to his core but staying was not a rational plan. He had clients, a business, employees and their families that depended on him. His own family would need him even more now that Amy and Rose were home. Life had become so damn complicated and nothing he was feeling made it any easier. Why had life dealt him a hand he wasn't prepared to play?

"Emma, if all goes well in New York I will be coming back in a few weeks. I won't stay away from you, I cant."

"Don't.......just, please don't August. This is why I needed a little time to myself. I just needed to release a few tears but now I...... can I just have a few minutes, please? I promise you I will be fine but I need to get myself together and I can't with you standing in here looking like.......heaven."

"I can't leave you like this Emma, it's killing me to know you are hurting. I want to hold you until it's all better, until you're better."

Emma stepped out of August's embrace and turned toward the shower wall. If she looked into his eyes any longer she would never be able to stop the tears. She felt the warmth of August's body leave and heard the soft click of the door as it closed. She knew the noise from the shower wasn't going to silence the sobs that racked her body but she couldn't stop them either.

Sitting on the bed, listening to the woman he was certain he loved, sob in the next room had him cursing the gods of fate. August stood on shaky legs and began to pack his bag, he was going to get dressed and take his bag downstairs before Emma came out. He couldn't bare to see the hurt he had caused in her beautiful eyes. Emma needed time and he was determined to give her what she had asked him for.

No sooner did his feet hit the bottom stair when all five kittens pounced and clung to his pant legs for dear life. One glance in the den at the older cats, whom he had come to know as Lou and Guido, and he knew he was on his own. The older cats were nestled peacefully in a hammock by the large window which meant the young ones were ready to play. Setting his bag on the bottom stair he reached for the kittens.

"Ok little ones, I will give you a few moments before I head out. You know you guys have a big job ahead of you. I need you guys to be good and take care of my girl while I am away. She is going to need lots of snuggles until I get back and I better not get any mischief reports. She is the reason my heart beats these days so you better take special care of her."

Most of the kittens were now resting comfortably on August's lap as he sat on the stair next to his bag. Cleo was sitting on his shoulder rubbing her head in his beard purring away. These little thugs had won August over his first night here. It was as if they understood you when you spoke to them. Although August was not really a pet person he was beginning to think these guys were winning him over.

Emma stood at the top of the stairs watching August cuddle the little mafia and her heart hurt just a little more. She heard him talking to them but wasn't able to decipher what the actual conversation was about. Not having August here was going to be heartbreaking but she knew she would heal, she had babies and a wedding coming. The boys would once again fill her with the strength she needed to carry on.

"August we should be heading out soon, have you seen Mikey? He is meeting us so we can drop off your rental and be my ride home."

"I heard him in the kitchen but I haven't made it any farther than this step. These little creatures sure know how to tame us mere humans. I will go check on Mikey after I place my bag in the SUV. You are riding with me to the airport, that's not a question in case you were wondering." August placed Cleo on the floor then gently removed the rest of the tribe before heading outside. As he put his bag in his rental he noticed Mikey pacing by the back door.

"Mikey we will be ready to take off in a few minutes, is anything wrong? You can still follow us and bring Emma back can't you?"

"Yeah I can but I am not looking forward to the ride home. Granny is going to be a mess, I just know it. Then I am going to be big time pissed at you for hurting her. I am going to want to fly to New York and kick your ass but won't because Granny will be even more upset when I get arrested for assault. I may

look all good guy on the outside but believe me, there is a bad-ass lurking inside that wants to break things. Especially when Granny is getting her heart broke."
Mikey couldn't keep his anger inside and since August was alone it was now or never to get his point across.

"Mikey, Mike, I can assure you that Emma is my priority and her happiness is what I will live for. I would willingly take a beating from both you and your brothers if I were to ever hurt your grandmother but I have no intention of doing that. I know I am the first man she has dated since your grandfather and I respect that. Mike you have no idea how I feel about her inside, I could never hurt her. I would sooner die a painful death than know that I caused her any real pain. Mike……I love her, I love her more than any man could ever possibly love a woman. I want to be the reason she wakes every day and the only one to make her smile but I know that isn't realistic, she has you kids for that too. I both curse the universe for taking so long to give her to me and worship it for putting her in my life. I am coming back and I will do everything in my power to make sure Emma is mine until my heart no longer beats. Did you hear me? I will love her until my last breath is drawn!"

"August? I see you found Mikey but…….." Emma's voice broke as she spoke, unable to form words. She heard most everything he just said to Mikey, it was all the right words at the very time she needed to hear them. August felt for her what she knew she felt for him. They loved each other, he loved her back.

"Emma I love you so much and I am sorry I told your grandson first, it should have been you but he made me realize…….its you that breathes life into my soul, not New York, not my work but you. Emma I can't leave, I don't want to leave. I need you, I need us Emma, I. NEED. US!."

August dropped to his knee and grabbed Emma's hand "Emma, I know I am a flawed man, I lose sight of the important things in life too easily. I take the life I have been given for granted but one thing I could never take for granted is you. I love you Emma, I know you may think it's too soon but I can't wait. I want yours to be the the face I see every night before I go to bed, I want to wake up to that beautiful face every morning for the rest of our lives. I don't want to waste any more time just surviving life Emma, I want to begin living it with you. Emma will you do me the honor of becoming the other half of my soul? Will you be my wife?"

Mikey was standing just a few feet away holding his phone, recording everything from August dropping to his knee on. He had never seen Granny look so beautiful in his life. Her face glowed and the sparkle in her eyes was almost blinding. It was in that moment Mikey was pretty happy he didn't kick an old mans ass.

"Oh August, of course I will…..yes!" Granny's voice broke as Nate and Rachel walked out of the house in time to see what had just happened. Rachel stood next to Mikey watching the recording on his phone.

"Mikey is that a tear right here on your cheek?" Rachel touched Mikey's cheek as she chuckled.

"No!" Mikey swiped at a fly as it flew by "Damn it, why is it when you swing at a fly does it have do a victory lap around your head?" Changing the subject from his rogue tear to the fly swarming his ear.

Granny laughed as August held her in his arms, smiling at her youngest grandson. Mikey was the grandson she was certain no man could win over but it seemed that even Mikey had a soft spot for August.

"Emma, come with me to New York to pack up my things, please? We will pick out your ring together and I can get my intern ready to take over my studio. I promise we can be back in less than a week. Please say yes, I can't leave without you."

"I promised Amy I would help with Rose while she works with Mikey. She needs to have her close and I have the kittens and Nate's therapy......"

"Granny I can handle all that for a week, I have to practice for this little VanByrne I have in here anyway. We are going to be fine, it's just a few days, go." Mikey and Nate agreed although they were pretty sure they were going to starve to death before Granny's return.

"I need to pack, I can't just go, I have to prepare."

"Nope, we will get you everything you need in New York. Let's get in the car and head to the airport before you change your mind. I can't wait to have you all to myself, even if it is just a few days." August kissed Emma and walked her towards his rental.

"We won't need you after all Mikey, see you in a few days kids." Emma climbed in the car and waved to the three of them. This was the beginning of her happily ever after, no matter how much life you've lived, there is always a happily ever after waiting, you just have to find it.

EPILOGUE

I cannot believe Uncle August left everything behind and came back here for Emma. If you are ever lucky enough to have that kind of love in your life what else would you need? Having only ever really known heartbreak, I can only dream to have a man in my life that loves so completely.

Uncle August didn't even make it to New York before he was begging Emma for forever. I would never have believed it had I not witnessed it with my own tear filled eyes.

The commotion in the driveway caught my attention while I was nursing Rose in Mikey's office. I was so happy that I got up and looked out the window when I did. I couldn't bare to go out there, my hurt was still too fresh but Granny and August deserve this, they deserve love. I had hoped everyone deserved love and that working for it made it that much sweeter, I was definitely wrong on that one.

Uncle August on bended knee professing his love for my bosses grandmother almost makes me believe in love again, almost. Even though Granny promised to be here to help me transition into working mother mode, I was happy for them. Rachel was amazing and it was really a blessing in disguise because she is a great listener too. Mikey was pretty cool about having Rose in the office and he even held her a few times for me. I just never pictured my life taking me here, where I am now, sitting in my childhood bedroom nursing a baby girl who will never feel unloved. I wish I could have seen it coming but life has a way of sneaking up on you. I have so many things to be thankful for but part of me, the part he broke that I don't think I will ever get back, isn't one of them.

So here I sit, on my full size bed with the flowered quilt my grandmother Rose made me for my seventh birthday, nursing a very hungry RJ, thinking about my run in with Paul. Why he monopolizes my brain I have no idea. He is at least ten years older than me and far more together than I am, but he seemed so nice. If I wasn't battling this whole fresh mom bod I would be swooning on his rugged good looks. That shadow of a beard and that shiny clean cut hair, oh and the muscles, dear lord the muscles. He must be at least a few inches above six foot tall, I swear he was in one of those Australian firefighter calendars. It doesn't matter, I am done with men. Life will be all about my sweet baby girl and myself from here on out, no exceptions.

"Amy, there is someone here to see you. Is Rose just about done eating? I can rock her for you if you'd like." Letty was outside the door to Amy's room waiting to come inside.

"Sure mom, she is done but she still needs to burp. If you want to wait I can….."

Letty burst through the door heading straight for Rose. "Give me that sweet girl and you go check on your guest. I remember how to burp a baby dear. Take your time, I will be right here rocking this child and loving on her."

Amy made her way down the stairs to the front door, seated on the porch was a very nervous looking Paul.

"Paul? Why are you here? Did I lose something else on my walk?"

"No, Amy, sorry maybe I shouldn't have come. I just thought, well I am heading to a meeting at the church and I was just um. I was wondering if maybe you would like to maybe go?" Paul was standing on the porch with his hands placed firmly in his pockets.

"What? A meeting on what and why would I want to go?"

"Well, it's just a few people who get together, drink coffee or juice with maybe a snack and just talk. We talk about stuff that weighs heavy on us. No judgement just people who listen, sometimes it's good to have a friendly ear to talk to, you know?"

"What makes you think something like that would interest me? I'm sorry to sound so bitchy but you caught me off guard. I'm just so confused."

Letty made her way to the door holding Rose in her arms. "Amy you should go, get out of the house. It will give me time with Rose without you hovering over me, let me be a grandma. I promise to call you if she so much as whimpers. Besides August and Emma are coming by to visit, you will be bored dear."

Amy sensed a set up by her mother but had no desire to argue in front of her daughter.

"Ok, give Uncle and Emma my love and make sure Rose is down by 8:00, keeping the routine is key mom." Amy smiled at her mother and kissed RJ on the cheek. She hadn't been anywhere but Granny's to work and the occasional walk. Maybe getting out would be good, maybe meeting more people would help. Being close to Paul isn't the best of ideas but he was really nice to look at.

"I guess I will go to the meeting after all Paul. Are we walking or will you be driving us there?" Amy took her coat from her mother, who just happened to have it ready and walked down the steps.

"We have enough time to walk but if you want to take my truck we can."

"You are kidding right? I need to walk as much as physically possible so I can get back into real clothes. Let's take the long route, I could use the extra steps." Amy smiled at Paul taking time to appreciate his strong features. There was no way her mom would push her out the door if Paul wasn't a good guy so Amy felt pretty safe with her decision.
Paul smiled but stopped himself from responding to her statement. Tonight wasn't the night to tell her how she made him feel.